(

Cover art by Howard Lyon
Edited by Stephen 'Shoe' Shoemaker

Chapter 1

Cilreth relaxed in her sleep web, eyes closed, reading off-retina. She pored over a report by Siobhan and Caden about Celaran cybernetics. The two had dived into the project with a vengeance, though the subject material proved difficult. The Celarans had advanced to the point where their circuits were built at a subatomic level, making them almost impossible to map and understand. Their software, assuming they had any at all, proved elusive.

She sighed for the fourth time.

I need to get the team another person. Someone young with a brilliant and plastic brain.

Siobhan and Caden were smart, but they were not ideally suited for the work. Cilreth wanted a new software specialist. Possibly to replace herself.

Maybe a five year old, she joked internally.

Cilreth finally felt comfortable working with Vovokan systems. It had been a trying time to arrive at this point of understanding. She just did not have the patience and energy to start all over again with the Celaran tech. If she stayed on the PIT team, it should be as their Vovokan tech expert and little else.

I'll put the new person straight on to the Celaran stuff. Though if they're supposed to replace me, then I should teach them about Vovokan software. Cthulhu's writhing tentacles, they need to be a proven hacker of Terran systems, too. Or do they? Should I start with someone who hasn't been exposed to—nope. They have to be a hacker at heart already.

The *New Iridar* was still en route to the second planet known by Vovokans to hold Celaran ruins. Cilreth did not know what they might find, but she supposed a return to Earth would be on the schedule after that. How hard would it be to find a new recruit? Did it have to happen with Shiny's approval?

Cilreth contacted Telisa and asked for a private channel.

"Cilreth. What's up?" Telisa responded.

"Do you think Shiny would oppose a new team member? Would I be able to find someone with only your approval?"

"I think we can take on whoever we want," Telisa said. "If not... I can add that to the negotiations."

Telisa still plans to deal for Magnus's release. I hope that's realistic.

Cilreth became aware Telisa had said something. She checked her link's conversation log. Telisa had asked what Cilreth was working on.

"Oh. I'm organizing what I know about Vovokan software," Cilreth said. "I'm going to quit the frontier once I have a brilliant young replacement ready for you."

"If that's what you want. But I really like having you on the job." Telisa sounded dismissive.

"I know, I keep saying this but I haven't left yet. I'm going to bow out eventually. Next time we get to Earth I want to find my replacement if you trust me."

"I do. That is, if you're not a Trilisk."

"That reminds me, I need to tell you how to run the check for Trilisk signs. Everyone should know."

"More than that, actually," Telisa said. "If the ship detects a Trilisk, then everyone needs to be alerted to my location. In fact, the ship should be rigged to poison me automatically if I get taken. We could use Maxsym's gas."

Cilreth did not answer right away. Telisa was a Trilisk host body, thus a danger if Trilisks came within range. Telisa just wanted to protect the team. Cilreth suppressed the urge to say she could not do it.

Telisa's being straight with me. She won't water it down.

"I agree. But only because I know you're a copy. We have the original Telisa on ice with Magnus, right?"

"That's what I've been led to believe," Telisa said sadly. Cilreth's mouth compressed.

Should not have mentioned Magnus...

"Okay."

"We'll need an expert for each race, I think," Telisa said. "I mean, I could handle the old job of pointing out valuable alien artifacts, but when we go tackling communications and software, we need one person to specialize in Vovokan tech, another for Celaran, and so on."

"I definitely agree."

"Then please stay on as our Vovokan expert. The new person can tackle the Celaran projects."

"I'll think about it," Cilreth said.

"We'll also have to organize what we've learned for our own knowledge base as well as for potential customers. We could consider selling some of it to the right people. The know-how is as valuable as the artifacts themselves."

"Maybe, yeah," Cilreth said. "You can be our Trilisk expert, seeing as how you practically are one."

"Oh, thanks for that," Telisa said, but her voice was lighter now.

"We could give away the knowledge of how to make Maxsym's Trilisk poison for free."

"We could... except we might not want any Trilisks left around to know we have it. I assume they could counter it easily, given the warning."

"Ah, good point," Cilreth conceded.

"Jason is the most junior team member, so he gets the Blackvines."

Cilreth laughed. "No one else would want the assignment. I haven't turned the lights off the highest setting in my quarters for weeks," she said.

Vincent had proved troublesome. He often crept in to any unattended room and started taking things apart. The team had learned the Blackvine avoided groups of people and brightly lit rooms with no place to hide. Everyone's quarters had turned into overlit Spartan chambers. They kept the alien mostly crowded into one of the cargo rooms with the lights out. The room had been filled with spare junk and empty containers to give it places to hide and plenty of toys to play with.

Efforts to communicate had not made much progress, beyond learning that Vincent cared only about Vincent and wanted to control everything else for its own gain. When any person or interface refused to obey one of its commands, it declared that something was broken and needed repair.

"Can Siobhan and Caden handle the Celaran side for now?" Telisa asked.

"Not really. It's not their fault. This isn't their specialty, and it's damn frustrating besides."

"It's good for them to try. They'll learn a respect for the job if nothing else," Telisa said.

"Anyway, I'll get back to it. When we head back to Earth, I'll find who we need."

"Sounds good."

Chapter 2

Telisa received an automated notification when the ship slowed its gravity spinner to enter normal space. She was already off-retina in her quarters, so she opened new panes in her PV and prepared to learn about the new system.

"The spinner has dropped us below the threshold. Rorka Cartur System is before us," Cilreth announced enthusiastically on a team channel. Data started to pour in from the tiny Vovokan ship's sensors. Telisa's PV filled with information.

The first thing Telisa noticed was that there was only one star and one real planet-sized body. Beyond the lone planet, an emaciated asteroid belt added a thin ring around the star. The system had no gas giant or primordial black hole to explain the presence of the belt.

I won't assume anything, she told herself. *There could be a space station here somewhere...*

Telisa looked for other objects of interest in the system. The initial reports came back showing a few small natural bodies in eccentric orbits. Cilreth started to devote more resources to scanning the planet, a decision which Telisa approved of.

A hit came in from the planet. One artificial site found... no others followed. Telisa felt a stab of disappointment.

Probably no active Celaran colony here.

"I see only one site. It's big," Cilreth offered the team on the shared channel. Her voice sounded more positive than Telisa felt.

Telisa zoomed in on what they had spotted. She saw a large flat area with some building-sized shapes in the middle.

"Remind you of anything?" Telisa asked.

"Well, yes. It's exactly the same shape and surface area as the large facility on the last Celaran planet. The industrial yard with the ship," said Cilreth.

"So another colony site, but this one didn't make it as far," Siobhan said. "I see the spikes and the vines, just like at Idrick Piper."

Telisa focused on the feed of the ruins site. The flattop had been put down across a wide field. The fence was up, exactly as at the other facility. Some building shells stood, alongside a few other rectangular holes in the field.

Standard operating procedure for the Celaran colony builders, I guess.

"Let's go check it out in person," Telisa said. "Start our approach."

"What do you think? Just land right on the field?" asked Cilreth.

"Do we really have reason to believe the automated systems will accept us again?" Siobhan asked.

"It seems likely," Telisa said.

"They had longer to get used to us at the other place," Imanol said on the channel. "Just dropping down from nowhere might trigger a hostile response."

Telisa considered it. She felt she knew the Celarans a bit already. They did not seem bloodthirsty. Yet, a blunder with the whole PIT team aboard could end everything.

"Let's err on the side of caution. Land just outside the fence," Telisa ordered.

"Got it," Cilreth accepted cheerily. The *New Iridar* descended into the atmosphere of the planet. According to several analyses, the air was very close to what they had found at the last colony site; given the vast array of Celaran vines growing across the planet, that did not surprise Telisa.

It's been Celaraformed; I bet it even smells the same down there.

Telisa watched the external feeds as they came over the site from above. Several large rectangular holes in the planet's surface had been created in the field. The buildings were not done.

Not even as far along as the other planet.

Cilreth did not see any unusual places to land, so she set the ship down amid the vines. It settled to the ground within 50 meters of the fence.

"Let's go," Telisa said, her voice calm. She knew the others would pick up on her lack of enthusiasm, but she did not care. She was already wondering if she should offer Shiny the Celaran spacecraft from the other facility for Magnus after all.

The team, missing only Cilreth, emerged from the ship and walked out into the vine forest. Imanol and Jason naturally paired up, as did Siobhan and Caden. Everyone had their weapons out, just like another of their countless VR training sessions. It felt good to do something incarnate, though. Telisa knew they would feel sharper, too. Ready for anything.

"Something went wrong here, or this facility would be completed," Telisa said, looking out over the vines at the perimeter. "I want to know what."

The others took her point. Had some enemy come in and put a stop to the base?

The light was brighter than before. It helped to remind Telisa that they were at a new colony. The spikes and vines made her feel like she had returned to the original site. The gravity felt heavy. Telisa accessed a sensor in her Veer suit with her link. It told her the environment was closer to Earth's gravitational acceleration.

Telisa watched the flattop and the familiar vine forest while Imanol and Jason cut a path through the fence. They walked inside on alert.

"I don't think there will be any Celaran guardians this time," Jason said.

7

Telisa nodded. They walked out onto the field toward the nearest building foundation. Telisa immediately felt vulnerable out in the open. She dispatched attendants to follow the fence around the perimeter, looking for danger.

Jason and Imanol led the way to the foundation opening ahead. They took a look calmly and waved everyone over. Telisa looked for herself when she arrived at the edge. It was deeper than Telisa expected; maybe two or three Terran stories down. One side was ramped, the other three were sheer drops. It looked clean at the bottom. Telisa wondered how it was that no rain water had accumulated there.

Their attendant spheres darted around the site like excited birds. They reported more foundations in progress. There were some construction machines, quiet hulks that had been powered down. Some had long legs, others had wide treads like Terran digging machines.

"It looks like work was halted a long time ago," Caden said. "I don't see any signs of attack."

"Maybe a factory was going down here," Siobhan said. She pointed farther into the field. "That one, I don't know. It's even deeper."

"Another spacecraft hangar under the surface," Telisa guessed. "It's the same dimensions as the hangar we left behind at the other ruins site."

Imanol shook his head. He voiced the same disappointment everyone else felt. "So we came here for nothing. No Celarans."

Imanol. Always with the light of the Five in his voice.

"One problem at a time. We'll finish down here and figure out something," Telisa said. She turned to Siobhan.

"Did all these materials come from the planet? I don't see any mines around here."

Siobhan pointed to the nearest open building on the field.

8

"That part there came from space, I think. A factory seed payload, Terrans would call it. I think this facility bootstraps itself with the payload delivered by spacecraft."

"So the spacecraft went onwards to plant a seed on the next planet."

"Maybe," Siobhan said. "Why speculate about that?"

"This facility was never finished, obviously. If they made a ship that pre-built these places, they would have it restock a new factory payload from here."

"And if that was the plan, then it never happened," Caden said. "So there's still a ship here somewhere."

"That could be," Telisa said.

"I can think of a lot of other logical ways for it to work," Imanol said. "First, you have probes that explore and report back on suitable planets. Then, these factory ships—"

"No, then the Celaraforming ships," Jason interrupted. "Then the factory ships. Then the colony ships."

"True," Telisa said. "Couldn't hurt to check before we leave, though. Cilreth?"

"Yes?"

"Take a careful look. Are we the only ones in orbit of this planet?"

"What?"

"Look carefully," Telisa said. "The Celarans probably know a few ways to hide that Terrans don't."

"I'm on it."

Telisa sighed. Her tactical highlighted an event. An attendant had gone missing. She frowned.

An alert signal came to her link.

"Everybody down!" yelled Imanol. Telisa heard a loud crackling she could not identify. It mixed with the high pitched sound of a laser rifle discharge.

Telisa fell prone with her rifle out. To her left, a stack of gray building materials set out in heavy blocks offered some cover, so she shuffled toward it. A quick glance of the field to her right did not reveal any enemies, but the partially constructed buildings broke up her line of sight. She accessed a feed of the danger through an attendant. She saw a bright light emerging from one of the most distant building basement holes across the facility. Much closer, a column of black smoke rose into the sky. At the same time, a light wind blew across her and a thrumming sound came to her ears.

By the Five this is familiar!

Telisa recognized the enemy. This had all happened before.

A Destroyer! Like Magnus and I saw on Vovok.

She checked Imanol's position. He was near the source of the black smoke, but the tactical displayed him as live. An attendant feed showed him covering in another of the foundation holes.

Telisa told her pack to release a grenade. She locked the device onto the target signature which was being refined second by second as they observed the enemy. More attendants dropped off the tactical.

"Cover!" Telisa ordered. "Release grenades on my command. Handing over target sigs." Telisa sent her target signatures she had developed for the Destroyers on Vovok.

We don't have Shiny's battle sphere here to protect us.

"It's flying my way," Imanol said. "I don't have cover from above." His voice was calm for a man who would be dead within the minute if nothing changed.

It was too bright for Telisa to get much detail, but the light could also guide the grenade to its target. "Grenades in three, two, one, release!"

Her own grenade spun off, accelerating hard toward the enemy.

Bright lights flashed across the field. Telisa saw more attendants had been destroyed. The bright lights and strange wind made it hard to stay calm. It was like fighting an angry storm.

We need to duplicate this in training, Telisa thought.

So far, no one on the team had been killed, but that could happen any second. Telisa put her smart pistol over the stack of heavy blocks. She told it to fire on full auto with one hand while she grabbed her breaker claw with the other. The pistol jumped around but it didn't matter: the smart rounds would correct their flight path to zero in on the machine ahead.

Booom!

An explosion boomed across the field. Then more.

Booom! Booom!

Telisa gathered herself. She knew she was faster than anyone else, and the breaker claw was more advanced than their Terran rifles. She grabbed a piece of debris from the edge of the foundation in her left hand and clutched the breaker claw in her right. She hurled the debris one direction and darted out on the other side of the huge gray bricks that shielded her. She saw the light from the enemy machine between two buildings.

Telisa sprinted into the wind to get a clear line of sight on the Destroyer. Despite her speed, the angles of the large buildings relative to her changed with agonizing slowness. Finally she saw the source of the light shine brightly through the obstacles.

She interfaced with the breaker claw. Telisa forced calm in herself and gave it the target signature. The adapter took only milliseconds to translate that into whatever instructions the alien weapon accepted.

KA-BOOM!

An immense explosion rocked the field. Telisa dove for the ground and buried her face under her arm. The light wind sharply increased into a shock wave. Tiny bits of rock or ceramic bit into her exposed skin where her arm had not completed protected it. Suddenly silence fell across the paved field.

She looked up. The light was extinguished.

"Cthulhu crying, is anyone down?" asked Cilreth from the ship. Telisa checked her team's vitals.

"Imanol, are you there?" asked Siobhan. Telisa saw he was still green on her tactical. She started to check everyone.

"I'm alive," Imanol said. "Half buried under pavement."

We all made it. Minus a handful of attendant spheres.

"Everyone, hold your positions. There could be more," Telisa said.

"What was that thing?" Caden demanded.

"It was a Destroyer robot," Telisa said. "A war machine from the race that attacked Shiny's homeworld."

"Then what are we doing fighting it? Sounds like our ally to me," Imanol said.

"In case you didn't notice, it attacked us," Jason said.

"I think it was shooting at the attendants," Siobhan said. "None of us were hit. Was it just luck, or were we not targeted at all?"

Might have been a mistake to start shooting. Imanol had to make a quick call, though.

"It knows of the attendants as its enemies. And we, by extension, might have been categorized as enemies. But you're right. It may not have shot at us until we returned fire. I still wouldn't take the risk, though. Imanol, you made the right call. Assuming that was your laser rifle I heard."

"It was my laser pistol. I shot back when it slagged an attendant close to me. At first I thought it was shooting at me anyway."

Telisa saw several columns of the black smoke rising across the field from the video feeds. The surviving attendants finished checking each open basement for more Destroyers. There were no more on the base, unless they could stealth or burrow.

"It's clear for the moment. Everyone, with me." Telisa stood. "Unless you want to hang out and wait for more of them." The others rose after her. They double-timed it back toward the *New Iridar*.

"What's with the name? Destroyer?" asked Siobhan.

"Not inspired, I admit," said Telisa. "That's what they were to Magnus and I at the time: the destroyers of Vovok."

"Any better ideas who they are now?"

"No. I don't know where that race comes from, so for now, I guess they're just the Destroyers."

"What does Shiny call them?" Jason asked.

Imanol laughed. He stomped his feet rapidly on the hard surface of the field, mocking the Vovokan's speech.

"Right," Jason said abashedly.

"Well, we know now they're the enemies of the Celarans, too," Caden said. They arrived at the fence. The net was still broken where they had cut it, so they retreated back out into the vines.

"Not necessarily. I saw no signs of battle," Telisa said.

"Yet it was here waiting. And something caused the colony to fail," Caden said.

"It proves nothing," Jason said. "It could have been their friend. Possibly the only survivor of some other attack or catastrophe. Maybe it even thought we were the ones who killed this place."

Well, he's coming out of his shell nicely.

"I agree. Nothing is clear," Telisa said.

And I need to think about this. Are the Destroyers really our friends?

"Cilreth, we're almost there. Then we're taking off. Everyone watch for more of them."

"Got it. The ship's ready."

Michael McCloskey

Chapter 3

Cilreth had the *New Iridar* ready to leave the planet in a hurry. She watched for the other members of the PIT team in a video feed at the top of the ramp. She could see the relief on their faces as they retreated back into the ship. The hatch closed and sealed right on their heels.

Hrm, there could be enemies here we don't know about. Like Telisa said, err on the side of caution.

Cilreth hit the crash tube alert in her link and increased the power to the Vovokan gravity spinner. The aliens had achieved cleaner, more efficient spinners than Terrans could yet build. There was less leakage to the vicinity, and the spinner took less power than its Terran equivalents. The *New Iridar* gently lifted above the vine forest.

She gave the warning twenty seconds to soak in, then powered up the spinner more aggressively. Her view of the terrain expanded as the ship rose. She kept a sharp eye out for signs of missile trails, even though beam weapons were more likely. Nothing threatened them.

Cilreth took a deep breath.

We could have lost someone today. By Cthulhu, we could have lost everyone today.

The *New Iridar* climbed into orbit. As her tension eased, she turned her attention to what might lay above the atmosphere. Cilreth told the ship to search for anomalies in the vicinity of the planet. She set various reporting thresholds lower than they had been for the first search, and allowed the ship to take much longer to sweep the surrounding void.

"Can we come out?" Jason asked from somewhere.

"Yes," Cilreth said. "It's as safe as it's ever going to get considering where we are and what we're doing."

She checked the crew locations. She could not tell for sure, but it looked like Jason, Caden and Siobhan were the only ones that had entered a crash tube.

That's weird, Siobhan wouldn't... oh.

Caden and Siobhan were still in the same tube and had not come out. She did not bother them.

Lucky kids.

A new anomaly caught her attention.

"Small oddity here. Maybe an unusual fluctuation in the planet's gravitic field," Cilreth said. "Maybe its mass isn't distributed normally..."

Cilreth pinged the area with active scans. Nothing came of that, so she compared active signals from the far side using a remote probe. The results were even stranger. There was something there. The *New Iridar* knew exactly how to classify the effect: an object cloaked from radar. The ship's computers put the object up on the shared tactical.

Cilreth immediately contacted Telisa on the team channel.

"Yes?" Telisa answered.

"There's a *hidden* artificial object nearby. Its course is not a natural orbit. Whatever it is must have a gravity spinner."

Cilreth focused her investigation on the object. It was large and complex.

"It's a big ship. Really big. We're in danger," she concluded.

"Stay calm," Telisa ordered. "Cilreth, prepare two contingencies: Emergency flight to the planet's surface, and an emergency exit of the system."

"As good as done," Cilreth said. "These Vovokan shuttles don't take much preparation. Not like the *Clacker*."

"How about fighting?" Imanol asked.

"Probably a poor choice," Telisa said. "It's bigger than us. Or at least, we think it is. We can't be sure just yet. In any case, this Vovokan bucket of bolts can barely fight."

Cilreth felt a very real tension. There was very little she could do to protect herself. If the alien ship proved superior and hostile, they would be left helpless.

At least the death would probably be so fast we wouldn't even notice.

"We've only ever seen a small Celaran ship," Cilreth said. "How can we tell if this is a larger Celaran or a Destroyer?"

"I've seen Destroyer ships, luckily from afar," Telisa said to her on a private channel. "And the *New Iridar* no doubt knows about them."

The *New Iridar* had not yet classified the object. Cilreth tried to force an identification. The ship reported that the anomaly did not fit any known signatures.

"Well, this ship doesn't recognize what little we can glean. I certainly don't know how to ask it about Destroyers in particular. Besides, if it's cloaked, maybe it can further distort what little we can detect."

Telisa appeared in the control room Cilreth had set up and sat down across from Cilreth. Telisa went off-retina for a few seconds, then sent Cilreth a pointer.

"These are Destroyer classes, I can recognize them. This must be the Vovokan marker for that race."

"I'm sending an attendant out there," Cilreth said. The *New Iridar* could release an attendant through small ports in its hull. Everyone waited while the tiny sphere traveled out into local space and approached the anomaly. Five minutes later, the probe neared the anomaly and disappeared.

"I think it's inside the cloaking envelope. It should come back—" Cilreth said.

The probe returned to visibility and delivered a batch of sensor data. Cilreth and Telisa pored through it for the next few minutes. The information verified that the object was as large as they had suspected. It did not match any of the signatures they had found for the Destroyers.

"Doesn't match, not even close," Cilreth sent Telisa on a private channel.

"I agree," Telisa said. "Of course, that race might have designed something new, but these differences are prominent across many categories."

"I see a lot of data from the attendant, but it's pretty crazy," Imanol said on the team channel.

"Bottom line, we don't think it's from the Destroyers," Cilreth told them.

"I suspect it's Celaran," Telisa said. "Its surface has some similar characteristics to the tiny ship that emerged from the hangar at the last outpost."

"Nice to have some good news, then," Caden said.

Aha, they're back. No need to let on I noticed anything I suppose. That would be so Imanol of me.

"What kind of ship?" Imanol growled on cue. "Obviously the colonists never got here."

"A factory," Siobhan offered.

"Maybe yes," Telisa said. "It's big, maybe it's the Celaraformer. And probably lots of other things."

"Can we communicate with it?" asked Caden.

Telisa steepled her hands for a moment.

"We're going to try for a day," Telisa declared. "Failing that we're going to investigate it up close."

"Everyone?" asked Siobhan eagerly.

"Well, you and Caden are the assigned Celaran experts. So you two are going in," Telisa said.

Cilreth watched Telisa carefully as she made the order.

Those decisions weigh more heavily on her than she lets on. It sounded effortless, but she knows what could happen.

Cilreth determined to learn as much as they could before the couple had to go out and approach the ship in the vacuum of space.

Chapter 4

"I get five attendants? Nice!" Siobhan exclaimed. The team had gathered near an airlock to help Caden and Siobhan into their space gear. Only Cilreth remained remote.

"Cilreth and I think the cloaking probably forms a curtain around the ship," Telisa said. "Within the curtain, things should be detectable. Once you pass the border of detection, you'll likely be cut off from us as the probe was. So you'll need to rotate the attendants in and out of the field to keep reports coming to us."

"Sounds dangerous," Siobhan said.

Caden and Telisa laughed at the excitement in Siobhan's voice.

"What? It's just that things have been... a little slow around here, that's all."

"Right. The firefight was yesterday, so you're bored again already," Imanol sniped.

"I said around here, on the ship," Siobhan said.

"There's danger, of course," Cilreth scolded. "The ship could vaporize you for getting too close. Or the cloaking field could cancel out every electromagnetic impulse in your bodies, turning you both instantly brain dead and stopping your hearts."

Imanol nodded. "I'm beginning to see why you chose these two for the mission. They already operate without their brains most of the time."

Jason nudged him. "You're going to feel like a pain conductor if they die," he said.

"I feel like one all the time," Imanol said.

"Enough," Telisa said. "I'm trying to prepare my away team."

Imanol and Jason promptly shut up.

"If you get in there, don't stay long unless there are live Celarans inside. If there are, you have my permission to stay as long as it takes to establish some kind of peaceful rapport. I figure it must be unmanned, though."

Telisa glanced at Jason. Siobhan understood her look.

He wants to correct unmanned to un-Celaraned and Telisa knows it.

Jason did not rise to the bait after his recent warning.

"That's all. Attendants first, in everything. We'll be watching."

Watching with a delay, if the signal can't come back through the cloak.

"I'll meet you outside in five," Caden said to Siobhan. She nodded.

Her five attendants spiraled into orbit around her. They gracefully synchronized their courses to avoid collision, yet managed to keep their flight paths casual and chaotic looking.

"Good luck," Telisa said. Siobhan nodded.

Siobhan picked up a real space helmet in the main bay. Her Veer suit had an emergency helmet, but since she had a chance to prepare, she took the heavy duty version. Caden showed up a minute later to grab his. They put on the large, round helmets and sealed them against their tough Veer suits. The helmet had a clear faceplate, but also provided a 360 degree view service, so Siobhan connected to test it out. She watched the new views in her PV. It was like having another attendant feed attached to her head. It would be useful for seeing to the flanks without having to awkwardly turn her head. For now, she anchored the view straight in front, as if seeing with her own eyes.

Siobhan grabbed her propulsion unit, a flat suitcase-sized driver with handles and three attachment cables. She snapped one cable on, then exited through the Vovokan spiral lock in silence with Caden at her side.

To action!

Siobhan referred to her tactical to guide her. Her driver sent her moving away from the *New Iridar* with one pulse of reactant. Siobhan concentrated on slowing her breathing. Caden traveled beside her.

"You're quiet," he said to her in a private channel.

"No, you're quiet," she said contrarily. They were both just distracting each other through the uncomfortable wait. Siobhan felt the familiar high of danger as soon as the *New Iridar* receded and she realized this was no simulation. At least not a known one.

"Are you a simulationist?" she asked Caden.

Caden laughed. "Well the way I see it, maybe life is real or maybe it isn't, but either way, it's not going to affect how I choose to live it."

"Ah, the cop out answer," she teased. Siobhan actually respected anyone with the guts to just say 'I don't know'.

"If it is a simulation, that means you're probably just an agent in my virtual universe," he said. "That should put you in your place."

"Ah, but maybe we're competing against each other. We suppressed our memories and we went into this VR to see who would live life to its fullest. No doubt we have some serious money riding on the bet."

"Maybe we did it to see if we would fall in love again from scratch," he said.

"You can't sweet talk me, mister," Siobhan said. She released a bit more reactant and pulled ahead of him.

"No racing," Telisa told them on the shared channel.

Caden chuckled to Siobhan. He let her gently pull ahead. She told her helmet's view to lock onto him. Caden's three attendants orbited him just as they did in atmosphere, except perhaps moving a bit faster than usual. It made Caden seem a bit slow-motion.

I'm probably moving slower, too. Despite our occasional VR training in vacuum, we're really not used to this.

The target on the tactical grew nearer. She quickly snapped her helmet view back to the front.

Any time now? Or will we actually run into something we can't see?

Siobhan prepared herself to decelerate relative to the alien object. The hidden ship snapped into view ahead of them as if it were the product of an instant teleportation. Siobhan smiled. The instant appearance of something so large caused an adrenal response.

Fracksilvers! That's intense.

Predictably, it looked alien. Hexagons formed most of the chaotic surfaces she saw. The *New Iridar* was a combination of many softer shapes, in the Vovokan style. As they neared the cloaked object, she got an idea of its size: at least as large as a Core World skyscraper.

"We have visual contact," Caden reported. "No doubt it's not one of ours."

There was no answer.

"Telisa?"

"Just like we thought. We're cut off inside the cloaking threshold," Siobhan said. "I'm starting the attendant rotation."

"Got it," Caden said.

One of Siobhan's five attendants abandoned its orbit around her and launched itself away from the ship. Siobhan locked her helmet video feed on it. She watched the attendant in the feed until it disappeared at the edge of the cloaking. The attendant would give its report to the *New Iridar* and head back in.

"Well, here we are," Caden announced. "Looks more like a ship than a station."

Siobhan studied the construct. It had near-symmetry along one plane she could discern. She did not see any reaction drive nozzles from her position. Cilreth had said the thing had a gravity spinner anyway. Its shape was wide rather than slender.

"Seems like it to me, but with aliens, who knows? Now to get in, if it even has crew spaces."

Siobhan let herself drift closer to the thing. The surface of the object was mostly dull colored, but a handful of stretched, six-sided sections of it were bright lavender.

"I wonder what these colorful sections are," she said. It occurred to her any surface feature could prove harmless, or deadly.

"They look like long triangles with the corners cut off," he said.

"Hexagonal. Feels very Celaran, doesn't it?"

"Definitely Celaran. All these weird angles like those houses."

Siobhan slowed relative to the object, choosing a course over its surface from five meters away. She gently jetted over toward one of the bright sections. Caden slowed as well, though he took his own path, increasing the distance between them. Another of her attendants rotated out as the original one returned.

"Let's try some other spots first," Caden said. "I see small hexagonal pieces up there that are about the size of the doors at the other facility."

Siobhan looked at the beauty of the bright section. She saw it had a regular pattern of small holes like a screen. Something about the color both intrigued her and warned her away.

To Celarans the bright parts could be the safest. If this thing is even designed to have Terrans or Celarans jetting around it in space.

"Okay, I suppose that's logical," she said, disappointment in her voice. She maneuvered her driver to thrust her in his direction. Suddenly, her attendant warned her of movement. She set the helmet's view to observe the activity.

Something approached her from overhead at five o'clock. It was a dart-shaped lavender object. She told her helmet feed to lock onto the dart.

"What is that? Heads up, something right there!" Siobhan piped the interloper through to their shared tactical. She magnified the view. Its pointy front had shallow bulges or ridges. She decided its nose was actually formed from several jointed legs folded together with the sharp tips joining at the front. It looked like a machine, not a living thing.

"Whatever it is, it's coming our way! It may be headed out here to slice us eight ways from extinction," Caden said.

"Then let's ride a tachyon out of here."

An attendant darted away from Siobhan. She assumed it would report this new development to the rest of the team.

If we die, they'll know what did it.

"We could give it a faceful of laser," Caden said.

We're out here in vacuum, without backup and hung out to dry at the slightest damage.

"It's their ship! We're invaders here. We got a lot of data and it's time to leave."

"Copy that," Caden said. He oriented himself for departure. "There's another one!"

They activated their external propulsion units and started to accelerate away from the ship.

Siobhan saw the one he had pointed out. It was uncomfortably close.

"It's coming toward you? Siobhan, I'm going to shoot it!"

"No!" she said. Her attendants interposed themselves between her back and the alien machine.

Siobhan felt a sudden rush. Additional acceleration. She pulled away from Caden.

"Caden! I'm accelerating!"

Her helmet feed showed the dartlike robot turning away from her. Another robot was behind Caden. She watched him move away from it as if by an invisible force.

Caden's new course was in the same direction as hers. Then the machine peeled away and headed back to the ship. Siobhan and Caden had simply been given an extra boost.

"We just got kicked out of the neighborhood," Caden said.

"One more reason to believe it's Celaran," Telisa said. Siobhan looked back. Caden and the ship behind her had gone. She was outside the cloak curtain again. Caden appeared as he passed the curtain before she could start to worry.

They tweaked their vectors slightly to ensure interception of the *New Iridar*. Siobhan smiled to herself.

Too long since my last big adrenaline ride. That felt nice. And it didn't get us killed.

They met their ship without any trouble. Siobhan and Caden re-entered the ship and met Telisa at the lock. The others were on a shared channel, but did not show up in person to congest the bay.

"I think it's a colony ship," Siobhan said. "Nothing more. The size makes sense. This ship lays down the infrastructure for a large colony."

"This thing, a ship I'll call it, has many layers of passive defenses," Telisa began. "I kind of get the feeling the makers had enemies, or at least did not want to be found by random aliens wandering by. If we'd been in a Terran ship, I don't think we would have spotted it."

"Why so well hidden? Why so mysterious?" Cilreth asked.

"To hide the colonists from enemies," suggested Siobhan.

"Enemies like these Destroyers you mentioned?" Imanol asked.

"Yes, maybe. Probably," Telisa said. "I think of a colony ship as carrying colonists. Seems like this thing comes ahead of colonists, more like a probe ship. My

25

theory is this probe was sent out to explore and seed new bases in far away star systems. The Celarans probably thought it best to stay hidden from aliens, at least at first. And maybe to protect their secrets," Telisa said.

"What about those robots that pushed us away? We need to get past them," Siobhan said.

"At least they didn't shoot you," Jason said.

"But if we forced our way past those machines, maybe the defense would escalate. They might shoot us next," Caden said.

"Those machines could be anything," Jason said. "They might just be repair machines or bots that transfer cargo around. They may not have weapons."

"The robots must have come out of the ship. One of my attendants is still back there, and it doesn't see them," Siobhan said. "At least it hadn't as of the last time it came out to give a report."

"Those robots are gone?" Telisa asked.

"Yes. The robots are either cowering on the other side of the ship no matter where the attendant flies, or they've re-entered the vessel. I'm betting on the latter."

"So what now?" Imanol asked.

"Just keep learning," Telisa said. "I'll study the probe ship's design and components. Siobhan and Caden will learn how to interface with it. Cilreth, Jason, and Imanol will figure out how we're going to bring it back to Earth with us."

"Are we both talking about the same probe? It's bigger than the *New Iridar*!" Imanol said.

"Figure it out. Don't forget this is a Vovokan ship, not a Terran one."

"A Vovokan *shuttle*. But I'll look into it," Cilreth said.

Siobhan traded looks with Caden and they left to start their work.

Chapter 5

After the relative excitement of the space walk out to the alien ship, the next day was an endless slog for Caden. He loved challenges, and always rose to the occasion, but instead of trying to sneak around an alien ship or fight off robotic drones, his task was to analyze software that they could not even detect running.

"We don't even know how to get into it... if it has an inside worth getting into at all," Caden said to Siobhan at the end of a day's study. She looked over at him from her seat in his quarters.

"The probe ship is hollow," she said. "I'm guessing from the energy output of the gravity spinner."

"Then it has to have a door or doors," Caden said. *Now here's something I can get my brain behind.*

"I have a different angle to work on here," Caden said. "Continue this without me."

"Caden... Telisa said—"

"To interface with the ship. Yes. I'm still in the ballpark, trust me."

"Okay."

Caden re-examined everything they had seen of the surface of the probe ship. The attendants had gathered huge amounts of data. They had readings not only from the visual spectrum, but from a wide range of frequencies, as well as more static EM field and gravitic readings. He spent the next two hours poring over details and forming theories. He abandoned several, then came across one that seemed to hold up to all they had observed. Caden sat up, re-energized.

Could it be? I have to try it out.

He and opened a connection to Telisa.

"Telisa? I'd like permission to conduct some experiments on the alien ship," he announced. "I'd like to use a robot to do it."

"What do you have in mind?"

"I want to try and get inside," he said. "I have some ideas how the doors work."

"What doors?" Telisa asked.

Caden brought up a diagram of the alien ship on their shared channel. He highlighted tiny grooves in the hull revealed by the attendants' many scans. The lines formed almost-complete hexagons at eight known locations across the surface of the Celaran ship.

"These thin segments of conductive material extend around the highlighted panels. Note they are not continuous, that is, they extend most of the way around, barring only one small part of each panel. That part reminds me of a hinge."

"How is the special metal parted to let the hatches open?" Telisa asked excitedly.

"I suspect it has to do with EM fields. I don't know exactly. I need to do some experiments. Expose these doors to field variances, induce currents, these kind of things. I'd also like to monitor them and see if any of the protective robots emerge through them. If that happens, we should record the EM fields in the area as a door opens."

"Okay, build a machine to go out there and conduct the experiments. Ask Siobhan to help if you need it, she's an automation specialist."

"Will do."

***

Five hours later, Caden's test robot was ready. It was a flattened oval with two cylindrical thrusters attached to each side. Siobhan sat next to him in a bay, surrounded by fabrication machines. The robot would have been a failure without Siobhan's help. As a frontier automation specialist, she had mad skills when it came to building robots from scratch. That had allowed Caden to focus on the equipment the robot would need to conduct his experiments.

"Let's send it out," Caden said.

"It's a bit buggy," Siobhan said. "But, yes, let's fix the problems up as they become apparent. If nothing else, we can whip up a model II here and send it out after."

"Telisa, we're ready to send out a robot," Caden said. "I think we should send a squad of attendants. I want to observe all these suspected hatches to see if the drones emerge from there."

"Sure," Telisa said. "Though the drones don't necessarily come out of the same spots the Celarans would use."

"Ah, but our Celaran friends love multipurpose things, don't they?" Caden said. He imagined Telisa's smile.

"Fair enough. Let's try it out."

Telisa came to their workspace and looked the robot over with curiosity. Then they carried the robot out into the lock, since it could only move in space. A squad of ten attendants crowded into the airlock with it. Telisa cycled them through with her link.

"And we're off," Telisa said. She stayed near the lock with Caden and Siobhan.

Everyone went off-retina. They watched attentively as the machines accelerated toward the alien object. Caden waited for Siobhan to complain about the lack of excitement.

"Not as fun as when you go yourself, is it?" she said. He smiled.

"So true. But I'm excited to see if this works."

The team of machines disappeared behind the stealth curtain. Caden had told the attendants to break off at any sign of violence from the drones. Otherwise, they were programmed to try to evade the Celaran guardian machines while other attendants circled back to take their readings. Caden fought with impatience as he waited.

Siobhan's predictable, but correct. Maybe we should have gone over there again, just to watch the machines in action.

The first attendant emerged from the curtain and gave them a snapshot of what had happened. Caden checked it off in his PV: the attendants were in place, the robot had approached and scanned one of the doors. None of the drones were visible. It awaited further instructions.

"So, let us know your plan, Caden," Telisa prompted. *Please let this work.*

"The attendants recorded some EM anomalies near these constructs I believe are hatches," Caden said. He was aware his voice had suddenly become more formal, so he tried to relax. "I see the same situation now: they all have the same pattern of fields around them."

"Could they be sensor pods?" asked Cilreth. Caden realized that the rest of the crew probably had little to do other than watch them. He felt a bit more pressure to succeed.

"The fields are localized. Not powerful, either. I think they control the hatches. At the very least, this is the field pattern of a closed hatch. The robot is designed to alter the fields."

"What now?"

"I'm telling the robot to cancel out the fields by the spots I think come apart."

"We're not in contact with it, right?" asked Cilreth.

"I route the messages through via the attendants that rotate out," Caden explained. "We'll try now."

The attendant went back behind the curtain. Caden waited yet again.

This is so damn slow. Siobhan must be going nuts.

He suppressed an urge to peek at her and stayed off-retina, awaiting the next attendant.

Finally it emerged. The next report came back.

"Nothing happened with the first experiment," Caden said. He became more tense.

"There! We saw one coming out," Siobhan exclaimed.

Caden checked her pointer. An attendant had caught sight of one of the drones emerging from the objects he had thought was a door. The drone was one of several which now played cat and mouse with the attendants. The attendants were backing off, avoiding confrontations, then moving slowly back in.

Yes! I've escaped being called an idiot. Now, to bring it home for genius status.

He checked the EM pattern on the door as the drone emerged and sent it to his robot.

"The signature changed when the door opened," Caden said. "We snapshotted it. My robot is going to try and manipulate the field into that shape on one of the other doors."

"Okay," Telisa said. She sounded hopeful.

The attendant slipped back inside the sensor curtain to deliver the instructions.

"What about the drones?" Siobhan asked on the team channel.

"I think we can come in and try the next step quickly, then run away," Caden said.

The wait seemed long, but Caden saw only two minutes had passed when the report came through from the latest attendant to rotate out.

"It worked!" he said.

"The door opened?"

"Not yet. Here's where we're at. We know where the hatches are. They're electrical. Not as in solenoids or electric motors, but at the molecular level. The material is sensitive to currents, or electrical fields at particular angles. By placing an induction device around the door, I can cause the sealant to give up its bonds with the door.

The robot saw that happen before it was shooed away by a drone."

"So now what?" Cilreth asked.

"Now, we apply the open signal and a simple mechanical connection should allow us to pop the hatch."

"Does your machine have that capability?" Telisa asked.

"Yes, the robot has a magnetic and a glue-based opener. For a last ditch effort, it has a crowbar."

"Crowbar? Now we're talking high tech," Imanol said.

"So now we decide if we should send the robot in, or go there ourselves," Telisa said, ignoring Imanol's comment.

"I propose we open a hatch and send a single attendant in. Then retreat," Caden said.

"How will it get out?" Siobhan asked.

"If it can't get out in ten minutes on its own, we can repeat the procedure to let it out once the robots go back to their stations," Caden said.

"What if we depressurize part of their ship?" Cilreth asked.

"It's not pressurized, actually," Caden said. "In the test, I relaxed the material sealing the door, but there was no loss of gases from the inside."

"Then the lock was depressurized. There could be another door just beyond the first," Imanol said.

"Maybe. However, our other analyses showed the outside of the ship is very cold. It could be very well shielded or insulated, or it could be an unmanned vessel that operates much colder than ours could."

"The guard robots are still in our way," Telisa said.

"I can get an attendant in there, I know it. We don't have to risk our lives," Caden said. He hoped that would sell it to Telisa.

"Okay. Do it," Telisa said. "Tell the attendant to run from any guardians. Have it emerge on its own quickly, if it can. Otherwise, we'll open the door from the outside again in *five* minutes."

Caden could hear excitement in Telisa's voice. She was as eager as he was to get a glimpse of the interior.

After the attendant goes in, maybe we can go take a look ourselves. If there's no deadly robots in there. Or aliens.

"We could go over and get live updates," Siobhan suggested. "Maybe check it out ourselves."

"Minimal risks. That's what these machines are for," Telisa said.

"It's ready," Caden reported.

The attendant slipped back inside the curtain. Caden suppressed a sigh. The delayed communication was so frustrating!

An attendant rotated out and sent them a report. Caden's machine was ready to open the door.

"Cilreth? You still awake?" Telisa asked.

"Yes."

"We can get out of here on short notice, yes?"

"Yes, ready," Cilreth said.

"Here we go," Telisa said. "Let it in."

The next report showed a video capture of the surface of the ship. The hatch had opened in the field created by Caden's machine, and the attendant slipped inside.

I hope they're not angry! That's a big ship.

Caden waited again. He expected the next report to contain video of the robot being shooed away by the drones that patrolled the surface. He opened his eyes and took a peek. Telisa showed no outward signs of anxiety, maintaining a look of endless patience. Caden suspected it was a facade, but truly he could not see any clues until she started to pace.

Yep, she's as impatient as I am. At least the robots are acting the same as before. They haven't gone crazy.

An attendant exited the field and sent a long stream of data. Caden thought that was a good sign. He dug into it, but Telisa was faster.

"We have data on the inside," she announced to everyone.

***

After a long and agonizing week, Telisa called a meeting to discuss their progress.

"So here's what we know, or what we think we know. The Celarans, Cthulhu, and the Five have done everything in their power to keep us from the secrets of this ship. We've worked hard and we don't have much to show for it."

Telisa referenced panes with diagrams as she talked, sending pointers to the PIT team.

"I verified details of the ship's construction against both the Celaran ground structures and the glimpse of the small ship we saw. We're definitely dealing with Celaran tech here."

Caden saw the panes she presented showed a series of common features. Also, the material of the small ship's skin back on Idrick Piper matched the dull-colored parts of the probe's outer layer.

Telisa shared a map of the innards of the probe ship. Data from various attendants that had entered comprised most of the map; the rest was filled in from guesswork. Not only had there been no light inside the ship, some kind of dampening field had tried to keep exploring attendants blind. The sophisticated Vovokan machines had responded by varying the frequency of their emissions rapidly. Some of the attendants had been captured by Celaran machines in the ship and ejected. Through repeated attempts, the PIT team managed to slowly gather a three dimensional radar map of the inside.

The resistance of the probe ship to their attendant incursions had stiffened to the point that they could not gather any more data without resorting to violence. Telisa had called a stop to the exploration.

"Our little friends have mapped out enough of the ship to show this huge space here," Telisa said. "Now, since the ship is Celaran, it can't surprise us that they like big spaces to fly around in. But see these patterns? These are stockpiles of various materials against this wall. Stockpiles that used to extend... all the way to here."

"Materials that it used up?" Cilreth said.

"Yes. It's almost out of resources," Imanol said. "We assumed the Destroyer was evidence the colony was stopped by force. And that's one strong explanation. The fact this probe ship is almost out of resources makes things more complicated."

"So it could have simply run out of materials to build with?" Caden asked.

"Maybe it's as simple as that," Telisa said. "I would expect the Celarans gave it enough to complete some number of colonies, at least every colony it starts, but maybe the Destroyers caused enough damage to keep it from finishing this one."

"You don't sound like you believe this," Siobhan said. Telisa smiled.

"I think that theory doesn't give the Celarans enough credit. If this is a Von Neumann kind of colonizer, it might have been waiting to be refilled with materials harvested from the planet before it went on to the next target. The attack may have prevented that replenishment, so now it's stuck."

"So it's useless?" Imanol asked.

"It ran out of *colonization* resources," Telisa corrected him. "Turns out, it can still run the gravity spinner."

"I hope the colonists received word of the attack and turned back," Cilreth said. "Otherwise, they might still be on their way."

"I wonder if a scout ship or specialized explorers came ahead of this one, or if this probe thing finds its own planets," Jason said. "I never thought about it before but there are a lot of sub tasks that could have their own kind of vessel. There could be an exploration ship, then a Celaraforming ship, then the base builder ship, and finally, the Celaran transports."

"Oh no, Mr. Classifier is at it again," Imanol said.

"Ah, but remember what we know about the Celarans?" Telisa prompted.

"Yes," Cilreth joined in. "They love to use flexible, overloaded designs with multiple functions! There's a good chance this thing serves as probe, terraformer, builder and colonizer all in one."

"That would be my best guess. So there could be tons of Celaran embryos, eggs, or seeds in there. Whatever new Celarans come from. That would be worth hiding and protecting vigorously," Telisa said.

"Should we bring it back to Earth with us?" Caden asked.

Cilreth sighed. "It's too large to be enveloped by *New Iridar*'s gravity spinner. We'd either fail to surpass light speed, or else we would rip it apart in gravity eddies and bring the pieces back home with us."

"How about programming? Can we control it, give it a destination?" Telisa asked.

"I've tried eight ways from extinction to figure out how to interface with it," Siobhan said. "Celarans don't use specialized processor components as we do. Their circuitry is built right into the materials. The only way we could even tell is by noticing what we thought at first were just impurities in the materials. Turns out, Celaran tools have controls built right into them at the molecular level."

36

"What about conductors? Insulators?"

"Conductive materials have insulated componentry inside. Insulators have tiny antenna lines going to the surface. Structures that have to be microscopically analyzed. I'm not sure they have software in these remote components. It's more like they have a software that designs how these things are made, then it's all hardware from there."

"But they're so flexible, software should be a part of it," Jason said. "Isn't software the ultimate way to make hardware multi-purpose?"

"Their tools are amazingly versatile, but maybe only in pre-planned ways?" Siobhan said. "They might be great at making a wrench into a laser and a fire extinguisher, but maybe every function is mapped out and can't be changed on the fly." She shook her head. "I don't know. They're aliens, after all."

"Can we get the probe to use its own spinner, somehow wire up our own control system to it?" Telisa asked.

"We can barely even get it to open a hatch," Cilreth said. "We don't understand the Celaran control systems... at all. It's not Caden and Siobhan's fault; understanding alien computers is inherently difficult. Remember, we've had Shiny's help to get us bootstrapped with Vovokan machines. This is a huge job and we started from scratch."

"We have to go home without it," Telisa said flatly. She did not continue. Somehow Caden felt her despair, though he could not see it on her face or hear it in her voice.

Cilreth wanted to ask. Caden could see it. So he asked.

"Then we don't have anything to bring Shiny?"

"We can give him Vandal," Imanol said.

Siobhan rolled her eyes.

"Well, could we leave him on the planet, at least?" asked Imanol.

"No! He's a sentient creature, show some compassion," Siobhan said.

"The lights are on in your quarters just as bright as in ours," Imanol said.

"I regret he's here, but we had to save him," Telisa said. "He was marooned on that planet. I just don't know where to take him now. Maybe Shiny will know what to do. At the very least, Shiny has the AI, so he has the resources to provide a good environment for Vincent."

"Cthulhu save us if Vincent gets to pray to the AI!" Cilreth exclaimed.

"He won't," Telisa said dismissively. "I'm going to give Shiny the location of the probe ship. It's a big prize. Cilreth, clean out the logs of any reference to the small ship we found on Idrick Piper. I want that one for myself."

"The attendants saw it," Cilreth said.

"Try your best. Supposedly they're *our* attendants. If we have to, we could deactivate them, put them on ice for our trip back to Earth so they can't tell him anything."

"Maybe we should leave them out here," Caden said.

Telisa was silent for a moment.

"Yes. Even better. We leave the attendants here to watch the probe ship. Everyone, we have to clean up any trace of that other ship. This probe ship, or colony ship, or whatever it is, this is Shiny's. We'll provide him everything we've scanned and learned, and he can come pick it up."

"It could even be good we can't take it with us," Siobhan said. "He has to give you Magnus to learn what we found where."

"At least for a time. He won't keep his word," Cilreth said.

Telisa nodded but said nothing.

Chapter 6

The *New Iridar* returned to the Solar System. Three months of time had passed on Earth in their absence, although less than that had passed in ship's time on the *New Iridar*. As the Terrans had advanced, so had the pace of their civilization; three months counted as a very long time in the political environment of Earth.

The ship's feeds were open to all. Imanol sat in his quarters, eager to see what had happened to Earth since they had embarked for Rorka Cartur. He brought up a strategic level map and tried to gather it all in at once.

I bet everyone is awake to see what The Shining One has done to our ancestral home.

Their Vovokan shuttle connected to Shiny's ships and began streaming huge amounts of data. Imanol saw Shiny had made more ships. They dotted the system, though none of them had approached the planets. They lurked on the outskirts of inhabited places. Hundreds of Space Force ships appeared on their shared map too.

"I see a lot of Space Force activity here," Cilreth said on a common channel. "Should we try to hide?"

"Yes. Just out of paranoia," Telisa said.

Imanol linked into Earth's massive tachyon receiver base, the center of all shared Core World network traffic. He connected to his news services and started to scan.

Ambassador Shiny? Blood and souls. Really?

For some odd reason, Shiny, as the new ruler of Earth, held the title of 'ambassador'. It seemed to be rooted in some initial misinterpretation in the days after his arrival, before it had been clear exactly what he had accomplished.

Indeed, Shiny ruled Earth now. The UNSF functioned only under his many heels.

Amazing. Earth has been conquered by a bloody alien tyrant.

Somehow the previous domination of Earth by the Trilisk seemed less real. Most people had not even known about it. The new situation contrasted that: Shiny ruled out in the open.

Imanol searched for the anti-Shiny sentiment in the network. At first he did not see any.

"Censoring the net, are we Shiny?" Imanol muttered as he sat, eyes closed, focusing on his PV.

Then he found what he sought.

Aha! Even Shiny can't squelch the voices of Earth's billions!

One man in Madrid complained that Shiny had mis-prioritized his son's birthday party. It was an incarnate event, and a large number of material transports had delayed guests by as much as an hour. Another person in Manchester said that Shiny had allowed his unoccupied summer house to go without maintenance and the roof had leaked enough water to damage some furniture.

"What? Must be a few complaints planted to seem authentic? Ridiculous. Is anyone buying this purple conductive paste?" he said to the others.

Imanol winced. He was starting to sound too much like Jason.

"This is crazy..." Caden said distantly.

Imanol did not feel brushed off; he understood that everyone was still processing their own discoveries. They were not ready to share, since it was too early for the big picture to emerge for anyone. It was at least clear that the others were as amazed as he was.

Imanol moved on to other topics. He verified what the map had already told him: The Space Force had more ships than ever before. The build up had apparently been completed. He read a story about how supplies for the Space Force were now being provided by Shiny from the asteroid belt. Earth was free of its burden of producing new ships and supplying them. Ample resources were coming in from the rest of the solar system to supply Earth. 'The days of shortfalls of any kind were over', said some bureaucrat or another.

The social entertainment scene was alive and bigger than ever. Imanol frowned. It was typical of Core Worlders to be obsessed with their virtual and incarnate entertainment. With robot workers bearing the brunt of dull work, citizens had little of meaning to occupy their time. It was an age of virtual world makers, entertainers, and leisure seekers.

Imanol's mouth dropped open at his next discovery. The top virtual social space of the week: 'The Vovokan Caverns, Location Seventeen'. A billion people had visited the virtual reproduction of Shiny's homeworld.

"Puh-leeeeze skewer me with a shock harpoon," Imanol writhed. "No! What has Shiny *done* to these poor people!"

"Imanol?"

It was Jason.

"Are you seeing what this incomalcon has done to our homeworld!" Imanol replied. "No one dares resist him. They can't even speak ill of him."

"Apparently he's neither incompetent nor malcontent," Cilreth said. "I have to say I'm finding some disturbing things. Ambassador Shiny is... well, he's the most popular leader Earth has seen in a century. Longer, actually."

"What? Don't believe it for a second! That bastard mind controlled everyone with his damn AI. Or something. He's a Vovokan snake! Blood and souls, I swear I'll—"

"Calm down. We'll do something. Telisa has to be seeing this all right now, too," Jason said.

"I won't rest until this is fixed," Imanol vowed.

"I'm going to go into one of his virtual adventure spaces," Jason said. "It's all the rage here, if any of this is to be believed. All my friends are saying how amazing it is. Do you think it's safe?"

"I bet it's how he controls minds. Go ahead, you be the guinea pig. I'll tell Cilreth to cut your privileges way back, in case you get brainwashed," Imanol said.

"Okay, I won't then."

"No! I wasn't being facetious. I really want you to be our test subject."

"Uh, thanks."

"Well do you have a better idea? I'm not connecting to any of this stuff."

"If he's using mind control I don't think there's going to be any dodging it," Cilreth said. "He wouldn't have to resort to any particular environment you had to connect to. He's got the damn AI, he could probably just wish everyone to love him and it would happen."

"Well it hasn't happened to me yet!" Imanol said.

"Good. Then *you're* our guinea pig, Imanol," Telisa said. "If you start gushing about him then we'll all know we're toast."

"You're not worried?" Imanol sent Telisa privately.

"I have lots of things to worry about," she replied.

"You don't know if Shiny will give you Magnus because we couldn't bring the probe back here," Imanol sent her.

"True," she replied. "I must be very transparent."

"No. It's what I would be thinking about, too," Imanol said.

"I'm making arrangements to meet Shiny."

"What should we do?"

"I'll have a plan for you soon."

Imanol went back to monitoring the news feeds and social channels. It would take a while to sift through everything, especially the explosion of stories right after the appearance of Ambassador Shiny. Earth had reacted with panic, then anger, then curiosity. From the outside, it looked as if Shiny had simply won over the population as a genuine liberator. But Imanol knew from history, there was seldom anything so simple and wonderful as a benevolent liberator.

Something else bothered Imanol. Memories of horrible creatures slithering in the dark had been haunting him. The temple. He checked for stories about the small island where he had fought for his life on his last mission on Earth. The search did not uncover anything.

Earth doesn't know what was down there, Imanol thought. *But I bet Shiny found out about it. Did he find another AI there? Is he using it to control the populace of Earth?*

Imanol knew he had to find out.

I promised myself I would never go back there. Blood and souls.

Imanol recalled that Telisa was making her plan. He decided he should ask her in person quickly. He left his quarters and tracked her down to her quarters. He told the door he had arrived and waited. It opened. Telisa met him.

"Hello," Imanol said. He found it difficult to meet her eye.

"What's wrong, Imanol?" Telisa said. She waved him into her quarters. He heard a surprising amount of compassion in her voice. He had thought she barely tolerated him on the team.

He cleared his throat. It felt weird to be in her quarters. As far as he knew, only Magnus had ever gone into her room, though certainly not here on the *New Iridar*.

"I'd like to see what became of the temple, and what Shiny made of that place," he said. "It seems clear to me Shiny is using some kind of mind control."

"And you think it's got to be Trilisk mind control."

He nodded.

"Then go there and find out what you can," Telisa said. "Take Jason if you want."

Imanol hesitated again.

"I have a... mental difficulty. That place really hit me in a bad spot. I think I could get in if I could somehow get a hold of a stealth suit. Just one person would reduce the chances of being caught."

Besides, how could I take anyone else into that place?

Telisa nodded. "I see. I got you covered," she said. She pulled a small sphere out of her Veer suit and handed it to him. It was a third larger than an attendant. "You can use my invisibility device from Vovok."

Imanol took the sphere. His link showed him it had services.

"You built a link interface for it," he noted aloud.

"Exactly. It's very handy."

"Thank you so much. This should help me immensely," he said. "I owe you... more than I already owe you."

"Get me some juicy intel. And, one more thing. This is just a loaner, got it? I'll pick you up a Terran stealth suit when I can."

"Oh, of course. Of course, just a loaner. Thanks."

Chapter 7

Telisa called a team meeting the next morning. Jason headed out for it early, eager to see what call to action their leader had in mind. Everyone had spent the day before absorbing everything they could find about Earth and what had happened while they were gone.

Jason had learned that Earth had been receiving a surge of supplies from Shiny, almost all the stifling laws of the previous regime had been lifted, and the populace of Earth was busy playing in cyberspace and incarnate. All VR time limits had been lifted, even for the Space Force personnel, who still 'voluntarily' kept their leisure VR time to a minimum. The Vovokan dictatorship also appeared to preserve personal rights and property.

Jason had found some dissent. It looked like sour grapes from those who had been in power under the Trilisks. It had not taken off like it might have since the very top of the food chain had been Trilisks anyway. The rich and powerful who had been imprisoned to allow the Trilisks to rule were apparently just happy to be released. They had not yet started to foment rebellion to put themselves in real power. He figured it was only a matter of time.

Jason arrived at the meeting in their mess. He took a seat in the corner and waited. The team trickled in: Imanol, Caden and Siobhan, then Jason and Cilreth. Imanol led off with a negative vibe. The others joined him: they complained about everything they had heard from Earth and Shiny to missing the huge size of the *Clacker*.

Telisa arrived. She looked everyone over.

"Everyone take off for now," she said. "Go wherever you want in the system. Your mission is to find out how Shiny got so popular. What's he really up to? Is there underground resistance to his regime?"

"I found some complaining, but it took me a while. Some of the people who were imprisoned on Skyhold expected to get their power back once released. Instead, they found themselves more or less like every other citizen: rich and free," Cilreth said.

"It worked out well for Shiny," Siobhan said. "The Trilisks at the very top are gone. The Skyholders missed their chance to whip up everyone against Shiny right away. Now every regular citizen is happy. The non-Trilisk leaders don't have any leverage."

"I'm thinking the Space Force isn't completely happy," Caden said. "Shiny took the system from them. That has to chafe."

"I agree, Caden," Telisa said. "I'd like to know what they're planning. They have a big fleet, though it's no match for the Vovokan ships. What do they want? The Space Force people have to be wondering what's going to happen? So far, they're hanging together, staying mostly out of the VR worlds the regular folks seem to love so much."

Several PIT members nodded.

What do I have left here? Jason asked himself.

"I'll stop by the PIT headquarters," Jason said. "Should we keep up that front? I mean, why pretend anymore? I think Core World Security, the Space Force, and Shiny all know about us now."

Telisa nodded. "Spin it off. Let someone else pay us for that business. They need to change its name, though. To me, we'll always be PIT."

Jason nodded. "I'll take care of it."

"Expect a visit from Core World Security. Maybe they're resisting Shiny. I doubt they would talk to you about it, though, because of your status as a team member."

Jason nodded. He looked at the others. Siobhan decided to go next.

"I think Caden and I are going to see his parents," Siobhan said.

"What?" Caden blurted. "No, we aren't."

"We are. Trust me," Siobhan said. Caden did not respond.

"Mend your relationship with them if you can, Caden, while you can," Telisa advised. "See what they know. Did they go from hating Shiny to liking him? Why?"

Caden nodded, though he looked unhappy. Telisa turned toward Cilreth. She took the cue.

"I'm thinking about taking on an apprentice of sorts. Caden and Siobhan have these Celarans' tech under control—" Caden snorted and Siobhan shook her head, "—but I'm going to find a computer expert who I can teach Vovokan software secrets, someone young and smart enough to jump on the next alien cybernetics challenge we find. There's only enough room in this old head for two races' computer systems."

"Find someone who can run and shoot, too," Siobhan said in an aside to the team.

Cilreth looked at Telisa. "I'm conflicted about that," Telisa said. "On one hand, PIT isn't large. On the other, do we have a place for a specialist to stay on the ship and back us up who's spectacular with the computers and little else?"

"There's a knee in the curve," Imanol said. "Find someone at least who is physically capable and we can train them up to at least mediocre. But for sure, the priority is strong software and the flexibility to learn something alien from scratch."

Telisa nodded. "I trust your judgement, Cilreth. Imanol?" asked Telisa.

"I went to an island last time I was here," Imanol started. His face pinched and then took on a forced smile. "I swore I would never go back to that hell hole. But now I have some perspective and I need to know, did Shiny find another AI there? If he did, it could be related to all this."

Telisa nodded.

"Good luck everyone."

"What about you?" Caden dared to ask.

"I have business with Shiny," Telisa said. "If I don't get what I want, then I'll join the rest of you on an intelligence gathering mission. I might visit some of my father's old Space Force friends, or... maybe even Admiral Sager. If he's still alive."

Admiral Sager of the Bismarck? We heard at one point it was destroyed. But things were crazy then, and lies were flying around.

"I hope we're not going to leave ol' Vandal on the ship by himself," Imanol said. Jason knew Imanol referred to Vincent. The name fit.

"I'll take him with me," Telisa said. Jason could hear the annoyance in her voice and he understood. They had all been so curious about the alien... until it turned out to be the biggest annoyance imaginable. The fact that it looked like a plant did not help garner any compassion, either.

The meeting broke up and everyone went to prepare for their trips to Earth. As Jason walked away with them, he already had another objective in mind.

I want to find the woman I met at Stark's. But what would I say to her? It's dumb to even think about it.

Chapter 8

Voss Marcant sat forward in a custom saddle as if lying atop a modern racebike. His pale skin clashed with the dull black of his clothes and the glossy black of the saddle. His pulse pounded in his palms where they rested on soft handles. His eyes were closed as his mind operated off-retina through virtual workspaces.

Marcant did not work alone. Integrated into his virtual environment, two other entities watched, ready to offer assistance.

"I think we're ready," Marcant said.

"We shouldn't be doing this," Adair said in Marcant's mind. "Let the Space Force attempt it. No doubt they've tried, but we could send them anonymous help."

"The Space Force? They have some good AIs, but their mindset will conclude that conducting a cyber attack on Shiny risks a continuation of the war. Remember, they're the ones that lost control when Shiny took over," Achaius said.

It was an exchange Marcant had heard a thousand times. Adair, ever vigilant, ever cautious, had been created for defense. Achaius was its mirror, focused on aggression.

"The decision has been made. This should allow us to get a snapshot of the entire cell," Marcant said.

"Some random cell, one of billions," Achaius said.

"Proof of concept," Marcant said.

"It might work. But if it's detected, your proof of concept will also be the last time it works," Adair said.

"You're worried about that?"

"No, I'm worried about what happens when Ambassador Shiny comes for us," Adair said.

Marcant sighed. Without a snapshot of a cell, he would be unable to learn anything more about Vovokan software. He had analyzed hundreds of thousands of intercepted transmissions just to get to this point. He had lined up dozens of variables in time and space to created a theoretical window in which he could conduct the copy.

"Achaius. Run it."

The technology of Ambassador Shiny was amazingly elegant and powerful. There were no handshakes, no separate authorizations, opening and closing of streams, or other complicated and inefficient wastes of time. In fact, it seemed so impossibly clean that Marcant thought he must be missing a lot of what went on. Nevertheless, he had a theory, and it had to be tested.

He glanced over at the captive attendant sphere that had provided him with about half of what he had learned so far. Its casing had been fused to the end of a heavy metal rod to keep it immobilized. One of his hacker worshippers had brought it to him; somehow damaged, the sphere could no longer contact anything at long distance. It remained chatty to its captors, allowing him to test many things without Shiny learning about it.

Achaius controlled the exchange. This time, they were not talking to an isolated attendant sphere, they were attempting to read data from a Vovokan shuttle controller. The shuttle was nowhere nearby; the test was being conducted from across the Earth. Despite the great distances and the many precautions involved, neither Marcant nor Adair dared to underestimate such an advanced enemy.

The request did not produce the desired result. Instead of a copy of a Vovokan data cell, they received an unknown reply. Achaius immediately halted the exchange and retreated.

"Passive monitoring indicates the last remote host in the attack chain has been compromised."

"He's after us."

"Probably not even him," Marcant said sourly. "It's simply an automated error follow up mechanism or security routine. We're outmatched."

"It won't find you," Adair vowed.

"Thank you, Adair," Marcant said, though his voice was sullen.

"What now?" asked Achaius. "Should we move on to the next theoretical model and devise an attack to exploit it?"

"First, let's examine the repercussions of what we've done," Marcant said.

"Hey jelly-brain, you're supposed to do that *before* you take an action," Adair said.

"Well I had mapped out what would happen if I succeed, which I'm accustomed to doing."

"You shot for the stars on this one," Adair said. "I'm seeing anomalies in many of our remote systems that should have been undiscoverable. Remember when I said it won't find you?"

"You mean ten seconds ago?" Marcant asked.

"Yes, that time. I may have been wrong about that."

"We may have lost over there, but if they come for you here, we have the upper hand," Achaius said.

"We need to take our obfuscation methods to the next level," Adair said. "Somehow the Vovokan tracking setup has made its way through all three peripheries and ignored all the fake trails. I don't know how that's even possible."

"So, he's coming for us now?" Marcant asked.

"That is a definite possibility," Adair said.

Michael McCloskey

Chapter 9

"Okay, so, we're almost home. What's the plan? Just introduce you, then grill them about Shiny?" Caden said.

"I can't just walk in there. I'm wanted by some powerful people," Siobhan said.

Siobhan faced Caden on the sunny balcony of their public skybus. A low power gravity spinner below decks turned the fat transport into a weightless island in the sky. They had chosen a relatively isolated balcony to enjoy the weather and the view without being noticed.

Caden saw Siobhan in his link as an artificial human, an android shell meant to be controlled by a human from far away. According to the ID, it was currently occupied by a man from the frontier called Carlan Jentaus. They had disguised her link to make it safer for her to come to Earth. The deception came with some small dangers. A lot of automatic safety features would not activate for a simulacrum. For instance, if Siobhan took a dive off the sky bus right now, it might not deploy a net to save her, since it thought she was nothing but a fake body for some paranoid sightseer.

"Shiny's in charge now," Caden said.

"The corporations are always out for themselves. I doubt they forgot much."

"I doubt they care that much here. Weren't most of your... misadventures..."

"Call them mild transgressions," she said.

"Didn't that happen on the frontier?" he said.

"Yes, but we're famous now. In a bad way. I saw many people asking about the entire PIT team."

Caden had also seen that he still had some Blood Glades fans searching his whereabouts. He had not dared to respond to any of them. That part of his life seemed meaningless now that he had been in action with the PIT team.

"I don't even want to talk to my parents. We're just going because you said you wanted to meet them," he said.

"Don't be an idiot. I'm just getting you back together with your family."

Caden sighed. "Well, you can join us later after I've felt it out."

"No. You show up with another girl."

"What?"

"Then I show up after we see what happens."

"Oh I see. Well, why just one? We'll hire several. You'll be one in the crowd." Caden smiled.

"Fine. You don't have to enjoy it *that* much, though."

***

Caden got on a transport disk once the skybus reached its closest point to his home on its course. He had been kind enough to warn of his visit, so his parents were waiting for him outside. His mother teared up upon seeing him descending on the disk. Caden saw many people in the long, sweeping house through several broad windows.

I guess they invited some friends and family to see me incarnate. How awkward.

He stepped off the disk and hugged his parents in front of the multilayered house. It felt weird, like he had re-entered a virtual reality that he had not run in several years.

"I was sure you would die," his mother said. "I'm so happy to see you again."

"Thanks for coming back," his father said. "I'm sorry the way we left things."

"So many people," Caden said. His parents did not say anything.

Are they hiding something? Maybe there are CWS operatives in there to get Siobhan? Or would Shiny let the Space Force pick me up?

"This must be Siobhan!" his mother said, looking over his shoulder. Caden turned and saw a tall blonde in a bright red and black jumpsuit stepping off another transport disk. He took a look around to see if anyone else moved toward them. Everything seemed calm.

"There will be women coming and going during my visit. Siobhan will be one of them," Caden transmitted to his parents on a private channel.

"Why?" asked his mom.

"There are people who don't like her. And me," Caden said.

"Don't like you? You're famous!" his father said out loud.

"Infamous, you mean," Caden answered, letting the conversation come back out to spoken words again. "I want you two to know, I was trying to do what was right when I went in and attacked those Trilisk admirals."

"You have it all wrong! The Space Force knows why you were there, Caden. All of Earth knows now. You're a hero again, just like after Blood Glades, only bigger this time. This time, for real."

What? Are my parents in a bubble? Or are they just trying to be positive for my benefit?

Caden glanced back toward the house and spotted four girls fighting to wave at him through a window. The word spread behind them. More people, mostly girls, started to move within the house, trying to catch a glimpse of him. He recognized most of the faces.

He followed his parents inside and was immediately met by four women. One of them, Julee, actually elbowed her best friend and stepped forward first.

"So glad you made it back—"

"Caden! Remember me?"

"Welcome back hero!"

"Caden." It was Cassie, Caden's old girlfriend from school.

"Nice to see you all again," Caden said loudly. "Don't worry, there'll be plenty of time for everyone to catch up," he lied. Right now, he just wanted to bug out and get away.

This is crazy. I just want Siobhan here. Then maybe these girls would all keep their distance.

He watched the girls nearby pushing each other aside to get closer.

Then again, maybe it wouldn't help at all.

Caden caught sight of a high ranking officer in a Space Force uniform. The officer was tall and fit. He had more hair than Caden had seen on a Space Force man in a long time, and a beard to go with it. He felt a jolt of shock.

He's here for Siobhan or me? No, surely it would be a corporate force sent to capture her.

The admiral walked over to Caden and his parents. The girls made some space for him, even though it caused them to push each other about more fiercely.

"It's an honor to meet you, Mr. Lonrack. I'm Admiral Sager."

Caden recoiled. "Sager of the *Bismarck*? That battleship was destroyed by Shiny."

"It was disabled. But Ambassador Shiny spared me and my crew." He paused. "The Space Force has never expected officers to go down with their ships."

"Telisa is looking for you," Caden blurted. Sager's face blipped. Caden could not tell if it was irritation or real interest.

"Really? I'll keep a watch for any queries from her."

"These must be your parents," Sager said.

"I'm Patrick. This is my wife Rose," his father said. Sager nodded to them. In the manner of many Core Worlders, no one shook hands. Even though no pathogen had decimated any large population for decades now, no one saw any reason to start up old traditions again.

"I heard you have a traveling companion," Sager said.

"Yes... she made herself scarce."

"If I may speak frankly, Mr. Lonrack. The safest place for her is by your side. The press is speeding here as we speak. You'll soon be surrounded by too many sensors for anyone to touch her."

"What? Why?"

"You're the most famous hero of the revolution, more popular than even Telisa Relachik in certain population groups," Admiral Sager said.

"Hero of the—" Caden started. "Wait. What do you mean, the safest place?"

"If any corporate goons come for her, or any deranged fans of yours are looking to remove her from your life, it'll help to have news agents all around."

Deranged fans?

Caden was still digesting that when Siobhan walked into the living room. She looked troubled. Caden motioned her over. She walked up to them stiffly. Her lips compressed and her eyes darted about.

The Admiral clearly recognized her. "Siobhan, I presume?"

"You're Admiral Sager. You're supposed to be—"

"Rumors of my demise and all that," he said. "I'll let you meet the family. Nice talking with you, Mr. Lonrack."

Caden nodded. The Admiral turned to leave, but he sent Caden a message through his link.

"One last thing. I know some good men, ex-Force officers. You might need an escort. For your girlfriend, at least, probably yourself as well. These men come highly recommended."

The admiral sent Caden a pointer.

"Thank you, Admiral," Caden said.

"You're Siobhan? I'm Patrick. This is my wife Rose."

Michael McCloskey

Chapter 10

A long ceramic dock ran down the side of the Aegean island where Imanol had landed last time he was on Earth. Imanol did not feel much surprise; it only confirmed what he had expected: a lot had happened here since Shiny arrived in the system. Imanol hauled himself up onto a decorative shelf of rock next to the structure and let himself dry as he watched. He had activated the borrowed stealth device before approaching, so no one noticed his arrival.

The dock station was glass and ceramic. The roof was the flat black of solar tarp. Several people moved about inside. Imanol tried to judge their duties. It looked like two of them were maintaining the boats within. He counted seven small boats and one bigger boat he imagined might hold eight people.

Why would they need boats? The island itself is tiny. For recreation?

Imanol tried to decide if any of those inside were androids. He expected that Shiny might not want any real Terrans on the island at all. He saw one of the men inside stumble. Could it be some kind of ultra realistic copy that made such clumsy moves to fool spies like himself?

Imanol resolved to get a closer look. He hopped over onto the ridged surface of the ultra hard ceramic that made up the dock. It felt so dense and solid, Imanol suspected if there was an earthquake or a tidal wave, the dock would survive better than the island beyond.

No expense spared. This place is still important to someone.

Imanol made his way past the various boats, none of which looked more than a week old. Each one had its own small bay with a set of clear doors blocking the way to the sea outside. The docks looked clean, though he saw no robots busy scrubbing anything. Two men had a boat compartment open so they could access machinery inside. They appeared to be servicing it, though Imanol did not know anything about the electric motors within.

A large, solidly-built man in rugged gray shorts and short sleeve shirt moved down the dock toward Imanol. He was moving slowly, but looked alert.

No way he would be this on the ball unless he got a heads up. I must have triggered something subtle he picked up on.

Imanol considered simply turning around and leaving the dock. Did he really need to know anything about this island?

Blood and souls.

Imanol looked through a transparent wall between him and the island. He saw a ceramic path leading to the center of the island. He knew any normal person would sneak through there and head straight out toward the hidden tunnel.

That guy will be watching carefully for more anomalies. The best way to foil him will be to take the most inconvenient, ridiculous route through here. Which would be... over the roof.

Imanol took a walkway out to the front of the dock facing the water. He walked out from under the roof and into the sun. He eyed one of the support beams holding up the roof, then started to climb.

Once gaining the roof, Imanol tried to move quickly. He did not know what sensors might be present. Despite the vibration dampening of the cloaking device, he still tried to step softly as he walked across. At the far side, he hopped over onto a tree trunk and came down on the island side of the dock.

The ceramic path led straight through a corridor of cleared vegetation from the dock toward the center of the island where Imanol had found the tunnel entrance the last time he was on the island. He had to decide between the vegetation of the island, the mowed area, or the concrete path. Each posed unique dangers.

Off the beaten path is tempting, but will they have sensors out there that can see me pushing a path through the vegetation? The mowed area is clean but it could have anything. Even mines. The sidewalk could work, but it may have sensors in it and I would have to contend with foot traffic. Ah, but I could turn that to my advantage...

Imanol waited. When he saw a man walk down the sidewalk away from the dock, Imanol intercepted the man and trailed him as close as he dared. He hoped any signs of his presence might be attributed to the authorized person.

They walked down the beautiful walkway until Imanol could see the hillside that had held the cave. Instead of the old root cellar entrance he recalled, Imanol saw a ceramic platform with armored elevator doors. Imanol looked for sensors. They were tiny, but present.

Security checkpoint.

Imanol saw the same large man who had come looking around at the dock standing next to the entrance.

That guy knows something. He must be waiting for me to go in there.

The man Imanol had followed continued on the walkway toward the area where the house had been. Imanol saw a much larger structure in the distance. It looked more like apartments than any kind of lab or factory.

Imanol stubbornly decided to outwait the man. He took up a position where he could lean against a stone in the hillside and waited, unmoving. The minutes ticked by very slowly, but the man remained vigilant. He was either pathologically paranoid or he had been tipped off to Imanol's presence. Surely no one could stand like that and watch, alert, every single day? Yet he did not seem to be an android. The man blinked, scratched, and shifted his stance periodically.

People came and went every fifteen minutes or so. It was just enough to keep Imanol from going crazy with boredom. He watched them go through the door or emerge from within. The people seemed calm. Whatever they were up to, it must be routine by now.

Finally, the man made some kind of decision. He turned and walked away. Imanol watched the man take the smooth path back toward the dock. Before the man was out of sight, a woman became visible heading toward the door.

Imanol suppressed the feeling it was all a trap. He saw that the woman carried two white boxes with handles, though she carried them stacked instead of by the handles. He waited until she came closer and fell into step behind her. She was short, with short black hair. Imanol stole a quick glance at her curvy body as he followed.

I have to take a look now? Some things never change.

When the woman came to the door, Imanol stayed close. She passed some kind of link check and went inside. The elevator beyond was large. Imanol assumed it served the role of cargo elevator as well as serving passengers. The woman appeared to have no idea Imanol stood beside her, but Imanol prepared himself for an unpleasant welcome. Being in the elevator felt tortuously confining.

The cell they throw you in when they catch you will probably make this elevator seem spacious.

Imanol was at least thankful that nothing so far had reminded him of the terror in the old root cellar and the Trilisk spaces beyond. This place had been cleaned up. He told himself none of the dank things he had encountered before could remain.

Finally the doors opened. There were no ranks of soldiers or security machines to stun or glue him. Imanol relaxed a notch. He stepped out of the elevator behind the woman to find the passage beyond branching off in three directions. The woman walked straight ahead. He tried to estimate where he had gone before, when this was nothing but a ragged dirt tunnel and an ancient hole in the ground. With no clear options, he decided to simply follow her.

They came to a round room with plain white ceramic walls. Two stacks of more white boxes flanked a round tunnel entrance. The tunnel was straight but long. Imanol could not make out its terminus, but there was movement within. Some kind of robot approached, but it did not alarm Imanol. The woman remained very calm.

A machine with a dozen legs emerged from the tunnel and deposited more boxes. Imanol immediately wanted to snatch one up and escape. He just watched. The woman put her boxes on the other side from where the machine had deposited its own boxes.

Are things coming or going? Or both? I have to know what's down there.

He waited until the woman and machine had left. Everything was quiet. No one else was around.

Imanol peeked in a box. It was filled with storage sticks. Each stick had a label on it with a 'requestId'.

Requests... for the AI?

Imanol knew the previous AI he had been exposed to accepted wishes or prayers from Shiny or the PIT team. Had the system changed? Requests coming in by memory stick seemed clunky and ridiculous.

Maybe they're detailed plans for complex items someone wants. I remember you had to know exactly what you were asking for, or else the AI took weird liberties with it.

Imanol left the boxes to head down the tunnel. Immediately a sense of claustrophobic unease took hold. If detected here, he would have no place to run or hide. He reacted by speeding up to minimize his vulnerable span.

Instead of light at the end of the tunnel, it became darker. He ran up to within thirty meters of the end. He saw a gray frame around the circumference of the tunnel ahead. Inside the circular frame, Imanol saw only perfect blackness.

A Vovokan security checkpoint.

He knew things had just gone from easy to hard.

Chapter 11

Telisa walked down a sandy corridor on one of Shiny's massive ships. Vincent trailed her by three meters. The Blackvine crept from one corner to the next, finding the spots with the least light. To Telisa the whole interior seemed relatively dark already, marked only by the chaotic clusters of glowing cubes and rods that made up Vovokan electronics.

"Broken," Vincent sent over its link. "Repair."

"This place isn't under my control," Telisa said. "It's not broken. It works the way the owner wants. This place belongs to Shiny."

She walked over a section of moving sand. It settled to a stop as she walked by. After Vincent scuttled over it, the flow continued. Other than the gentle white noise of the moving sand, there was no noise. Up ahead, the sand became tightly packed. Telisa did not know what that meant. She knew the sand floor carried away debris. What did it mean when the floor became firm?

Shiny awaited them in a large chamber. Telisa walked boldly forward but Vincent hung back.

Probably afraid of this bright creature, Telisa guessed. *Maybe I should be afraid now, too. Shiny is Sol's dictator. Will he act differently?*

Shiny said nothing, so Telisa spoke first.

"I've returned," she said. "The PIT team found Celaran bases, machines, and a starship."

"Shiny familiar with Terran convention, habit, method of stating obvious. Congratulations forwarded for successful, fruitful, productive mission."

She waited for Shiny to ask about his dead battle machine.

"Artifact list examined, noted, processed. Telisa craft does not contain alien starship."

"We couldn't control it, even though it was unmanned and apparently without purpose. Its colony-establishing resources were exhausted as far as we could tell. It was large, maybe a third the mass of this ship."

"Telisa and team unable to deliver, produce, hand over starship? Telisa's recovery of partner, friend, lover Magnus requires—"

"I'll give you the location if you release Magnus to rejoin my team," Telisa said. "Our effectiveness was greatly reduced without him. I want to go back and find the Celarans. We need him."

Telisa sent Shiny a pointer.

"Shiny will consider, weigh, ponder this offer," he said.

Do I dare hope?

"I have other important information I offer for free. We met a Destroyer. Like the machines that destroyed Vovok. There was only one, or we might have been killed. We need more resources, a better ship, and most of all, we need Magnus back."

Telisa remembered when she had first met Magnus. He was strong and exuded a confidence she could only feign. 'A military advisor to the team', he had called himself.

"He has more combat experience than the rest of us," Telisa said. "He taught me how to fight. If we're going to encounter more of these Destroyers, we need him. He'll construct more combat robots to support our efforts."

"Shiny adds Telisa's new facts, opinions, variables to consideration process."

Vincent had shambled to one side of the room to investigate Vovokan cybernetics embedded in the wall there. The Blackvine started to dig into the sand with its tendrils.

"My companion here is Vincent. We call his race Blackvine. Do you know about it?"

"This race, species, type possesses Vovokan name," Shiny said. "Antisocial, isolated, intractable to trade, barter, agreements. Known to be tolerated, accepted, ignored by Celarans."

Aha. So that's why we found them on the habitat and the Celaran colony. If the Celarans tolerated this, then they must be peaceful indeed.

"Surely the Vovokans were able to enslave them, too?" Telisa asked pointedly. As she expected, her barb was either ignored or lost on the Vovokan.

"No social order, structure, framework. Atrophied tools for communication. This race not helpful, cooperative, useful."

"Well you have that right. There's no place for it on my crew. Vincent has been nothing but trouble the whole voyage back. We tried to communicate, tried to cooperate, but nothing worked."

Telisa spoke the truth. The Blackvine had been constantly experimenting, stealing, and vandalizing things during the voyage. The rest of the PIT team had developed methods of isolating themselves and their property from the alien. Even though it was supposed to be one of the insane Blackvines, it remained reclusive.

"Shiny can place creature in isolation for study."

"Study as in carve up or study as in observe?"

"Observe, experiment, learn, then place in stasis."

Telisa considered the offer. Some part of her felt it was wrong to simply turn over Vincent to Shiny, but her practical side had had it with the creature. They had wasted so much time trying to get through to Vincent without success. Telisa needed to focus on the Celarans and getting Magnus back. She did not find much pity for the Blackvine. She struggled with the guilt for only a moment longer.

There's only so many things I can work on, so many things I can fix at once in the universe. I can't even ask it where it wants to go, what it wants to do.

"Okay, take it," she said. "Though I would prefer you transport it to the space habitat with the other ones we found, I have nothing to offer for the deal."

Shiny said nothing, so Telisa continued.

"I have some questions about recent events."

"Standing by, waiting, blocked on Telisa."

"Ambassador Shiny? Who came up with that one?"

"Celebrity, activist, thought leader Sterla Molde."

Telisa's eyebrow rose. That was a more direct answer than she had anticipated.

"You're using the AI to make my race happy to have you as their dictator," Telisa said.

"Negative, incorrect, inaccurate. Shiny utilizing the system optimally. It is Shiny's desire, plan, best interest to keep Terran population happy, content, satiated."

"No way. They went from screaming alien invasion to singing your praises."

"Terrans anxious in face of change. Change proven, shown to be, turned out beneficial to Terrans. Terrans express relief, appreciation, admiration."

Telisa raised an eyebrow.

"I need to augment my team. My people will rest for a while, then we'll go back out. I assume I have your support to hire whoever I need?"

"Shiny pays, provides, foots the bill. Telisa explores, discovers, locates, and returns valuable technologies."

"Let me know when you decide about Magnus."

"Affirmative, agreed, will do."

Telisa frowned. Shiny's synthetic voice sounded all too happy.

Chapter 12

Hours after everyone else had left the *New Iridar*, Cilreth worked to finish off her list of candidates and form a travel plan to visit all of them efficiently. A message came into her link.

It was from Shiny.

"Shiny observed, noted, discovered Cilreth seeks self-replacement. Possible goal to staff PIT team with new expert. Recommended course of action, investigation, inquiry: Marcant. Subject has hacked, tested, challenged Shiny electronic defenses. Indicates strong, bold, fearless curiosity and technical aptitude, capability, prowess."

"Cthulhu sleeps," Cilreth said to herself. How could Shiny have discerned her purpose so quickly?

Cilreth reminded herself how powerful the alien had become.

So what did Shiny have to gain? Did he send her on an errand to find this Marcant, just so Shiny could eliminate him?

Shiny is so powerful, it seems like he could find and vanish anyone he wanted without my help.

"So I guess I find this Marcant. Am I supposed to reply or what?" she asked herself.

She decided not to. If Shiny was omniscient now, he would track all her movements and know about everything she did anyway.

Marcant. Just a first name. Or is it a last name? Billions of people and he sends me one word?

Cilreth immersed herself in the Terran network and brought out the tools of her previous job as a tracker. She knew how to find lost people, even people who wanted to stay lost. Within ten minutes she realized the name Marcant had very special meaning attached to it here on Earth: Marcant was the name of an infamous hacker. In ten more minutes she realized *infamous* was only the right word if you were on the side of the Core World government. If you were an average citizen, Marcant meant someone who stood for the people. Marcant had been fighting against the Trilisks in his own way, though whether or not he had understood he fought aliens, Cilreth did not yet know.

Marcant had quite a following. No authoritative sources of information about him seemed to exist, though the Earthers had plenty to say about him. The material she found was wildly contradictory and sensationalized.

There probably is no Marcant. Shiny just wants me to waste my time? This could be nothing more than a legend. A fake target put up to draw fire.

Cilreth took a deep breath and went back on-retina. She frowned. Shiny had no reason to sabotage her search for real candidates, did he? The PIT team was out at his behest searching for alien technology. Cilreth sent her attendant out to retrieve food and started again.

If Marcant is real, I can find him.

She started to set her search in motion. She had a new edge since she had last done this: the *New Iridar* had plenty of computing horsepower all on its own. She did not need to draw on as many external resources to help out.

Marcant had several layers of protection. First, who knew what activities the computers of Earth performed at his command? She started to accumulate the suppositions of billions on the goals, activities, and identities of Marcant. The bulk of the information was bound to be wrong, but Cilreth knew how to grade and weight sources of information by finding out how accurate other information provided by those sources was. There were also sources for hire with extremely high accuracy ratings that got high prices based upon their reliability. Hours flew by while Cilreth worked.

A general picture emerged of a cluster of incidents and agents believed to belong to Marcant across all of Earth. Like anyone trying to hide his or her activity and identity on the network, this entity used an obfuscation service. But it wasn't a commercial obfuscation service like any average citizen could buy. It was something black market.

Or more likely, something controlled completely by Marcant himself or herself... or itself.

Cilreth remembered her encounters with strange entities like GoliathFive that had helped her with the smart filter she needed back when she worked with Telisa's father. Maybe Marcant was not Terran at all. At least not a walking, talking collection of biological cells.

Cilreth came up with a "short" list of a hundred individuals she believed could be Marcant. The association with Marcant and this group meant that even if any one of them was not Marcant, they might well be working with or for Marcant. They would be a good place to start the incarnate part of her mission.

Cilreth requested a connection with Telisa. It went through immediately.

"Telisa?"

"Yes?"

"Shiny recommended a candidate to me. A guy who tried to hack him."

"Hrm. Your discretion," Telisa said.

"It could be a way for Shiny to—you know—more subtly replace the combat sphere."

"He would be more subtle, alright."

"Well you know, he's gone meta, right up front is the new subtle," Cilreth continued.

"Why did you call me if—" Telisa said.

"Yes, yes, okay, I just wanted to let you know. I haven't decided, obviously."

"Okay. I trust you."

"Any idea what security is like now with the new government? Everyone is saying it's greatly reduced," Cilreth said.

"Take a weapon."

"Screw it. I'm an agent of Shiny now. I guess I'll do whatever I want."

"Ah, how quickly power corrupts," Telisa remarked.

"Exactly."

Chapter 13

Jason returned to PIT headquarters in a light Denver rain. His one-person conveyance shuddered to a halt at the curb before their building. He stepped out.

The air smelled of the green grass before him. It had grown to its full height of 10 centimeters, forming a thick bed of green beside the walkway. Jason looked over the grounds with an eye toward finding any neglected maintenance. It all looked in order.

News drones hovered overhead. Several of them descended to intercept him like an automated attack squadron. Jason felt a sudden urge to drop prone and go for his weapon. Then he smiled.

I'm starting to become a frontiersman, after all.

The drones fell into a line. The winner addressed Jason first.

"DW news. Is Telisa Relachik in-system? Is she expected here soon?"

Jason decided he could answer a few questions on his way in. He started off for the sanctuary of the main building.

"She's not coming here," Jason said. *Why do you care?*

The drone dropped out of the line which was following Jason. The next one shot forward.

"AR events channel. Is Caden Lonrack alive? Follow up: is he in-system?"

Jason's face twitched in exasperation. "Caden is in-system and alive."

The drone swapped out. Jason estimated he would have to talk to one more before he made it inside. He made a beeline for the main doors. A few people were getting out of taxis down the street and hurrying over toward the PIT building.

"Jackson Action Reporting. Jason, have you met with Ambassador Shiny incarnate since arriving back at Sol?"

Jason took a deep breath to consume another second. "No, I have not met with Shiny recently."

Damn. I should not have added that 'recently' part.

The doors opened. Jason stepped inside, leaving the news drones outside, and found himself confronted by an entirely different army. Six men and women in various forms of affluent dress stood as he entered the lobby. They charged in a two-dimensional version of the drone rush that had happened outside. A tall man with short black hair took the lead and spoke first.

"You're Jason Yang. The team is back at Sol? What are you doing next? I want to book a mission with the team."

"Hello sir," Jason said. "I believe you have me at a disadvantage."

"I'm your highest paying customer! I've earned—"

"No, you aren't!" someone objected.

"I *will be* your highest paying customer when you let me join the PIT team!" an older woman shrilled from the back.

Jason held up his hands.

"I'm here to finish my last bit of business with Parker Interstellar Travels," he told them. "The company is to be put up for sale. We simply have too many other complex matters to address to be able to give this agency the attention it deserves."

"I'm buying. If you take me on an adventure with you," a tall blonde woman said. Jason forced his eyes to slide over her statuesque body in an instant, lest his gaze become rude.

"We?" someone else said. "Is Telisa Relachik also selling her interest in the company?"

"I'm sorry but the team has all the members it needs at the moment," Jason lied. "Yes, Telisa is cutting her ties with this agency."

"Why would she do that?" someone asked.

"Why would anyone settle for anything less? It'll be just another travel agency then," someone else said.

"She has more important things to do!" someone declared.

"Saving us from aliens?" a male voice asked.

"Finding the aliens!" said the tall blonde.

"I'm sorry everyone. You'll have to contact the new owners," Jason said, letting himself into the private area of the headquarters. Jason closed the door and leaned against it. He went briefly off-retina to check the estate's security arrangements. He increased their security budget and offered it up to their current provider. A flood of takeover bids came in from other security agencies. The counter offers were low; some were free.

They all want to guard us. For the publicity.

"May they sleep with Cthulhu!" he said, wiping sweat from his neck. "This place is insane."

"Can I get you a drink?"

The voice was familiar. Jason opened his eyes and saw an android wearing Thomas's face.

"Ah, Thomas. Thank you for your service. Please find Jack and tell him to deactivate. Then do the same. I think our days of avoiding Core World security are... well, our ruse has long been seen through at this point."

Biggest understatement ever. I wouldn't be surprised if both androids are compromised by now, anyway, Jason thought. He moved to his upstairs office to conduct more business.

Jason started putting out feelers for interested buyers. Despite what had been said outside, there would be plenty of entrepreneurs ready to milk the old PIT agency for all it was worth, even if their contract required choosing a different name. He had several tour captains out to various places on the frontier now. They would finish their tours and come back without cutting anything short. Jason did not need to wait for them to come back, though. It could all be written into the agreement.

Jason did a last bit of checking on the official records of the front company. Everything illegal had been compartmentalized and handled by Jack, then Telisa, so most everything had already been cleaned. It had been part of his job to make sure the records were as mundane as possible when he was working here.

It felt strange to walk through the headquarters again, as if his adventures had been nothing but a dream.

Strange but good, he thought. *I'm not giving up this new life.*

A loud crash erupted from downstairs, toward the front lobby. Then the roar of dozens of yammering people flooded upwards. Jason checked a video feed from the front office. Huge numbers of customers streamed in. Some were climbing through window frames that had been breached.

All the crazies coming out of the woodwork.

Jason's heart rate increased. Once again he felt like reaching for weapons.

A dozen news agencies entreated his link for comments on the current riot brewing at PIT agency headquarters. They joined those seeking to buy the company and those wanted to handle the security in his link's waiting queue.

Riot. I underestimated how famous we've become since the Trilisks were ousted.

Jason scrambled the interior map service and took his own office completely off the map display. Then he closed his door.

"Thomas! Jack!" Jason called. No response came. He re-activated the androids with his link and ordered them to try and keep the crowd back.

That's not going to work! I need real security!

Jason called out for help on the network with an offer for rapid security response. The offer was accepted instantly. Jason felt first relief, then confusion as he saw the name: VPSF. Vovokan Physical Security Forces.

Shiny has security forces on Earth? What are these, Vovokan brownshirts?

He spent the next minute trying to figure out how to barricade his office with a faux wood desk that weighed hardly anything. As he tried to decide whether to hide or seal himself in further, attendants whirled into the office through a window and located him.

He heard unpleasant noises outside, then screaming and yelling. Jason checked his outside sensor feeds. People were staggering away from the PIT building, driven by gas and sonics.

"VPSF? I just want to clean out my things and leave this place," Jason said.

"An air shuttle is being dispatched. Come to the roof, if you please."

Jason gathered a few personal items and the agency's onsite datastore cylinder, then he opened a maintenance door in the ceiling and took its lift to the roof.

Michael McCloskey

Chapter 14

"I've received an invitation from Admiral Sager," Caden said. Jason had provided him a temporary apartment outside Denver which he shared with Siobhan. So far no one had sold out their location, though Caden was half holding his breath, waiting for something bad to happen.

"Sager? It's a trap!" Siobhan said.

"I don't think so. It's in the news. They intend to award me."

"What?!"

"Everyone loves Ambassador Shiny and they know about the Trilisks now. Those people on Skyhold have been let loose, and they hold a lot of influence. Everyone knows what I did and why."

Siobhan shook her head and sat down beside him.

"It's so confusing. I don't know what to think about any of this."

"For now just accept it. Keep your eyes and ears open. We need to find out if anything is behind it. Trilisks, Vovokans... anything. Telisa wants us to learn first, then we'll act."

Siobhan nodded her head. "Do you go alone?"

"Yes. But I won't be gone long."

Caden watched her carefully. She seemed to accept his decision to go. She did not seem angry that the invitation was for him alone. He went to the window and took a look from his vantage point at the corner of a high building. Down below, he saw a familiar looking sphere patrolling the area.

Caden brought up a link connection. "Shiny? Why are there Vovokan battle spheres outside my apartment?"

"Terran homeworld crowds are unsafe, unpredictable, volatile. Many wish your mate, partner, girlfriend to come to harm."

"You're selling to me that this battle sphere, a war machine, is here to protect Siobhan?"

"Correct, affirmative, verified."

Caden turned to Siobhan.

"Good news is you'll be safe. Shiny has some slickblack security around here."

"What? For me?"

"He's keeping the peace, or whatever. I'm so sorry this has happened. Of course I never wanted to be branded a traitor, but this is over the top the other direction."

"I like it."

Now it was Caden's turn to be surprised. "You do?"

Siobhan embraced him. She held his face and looked down on him. "All those girls want you, but you're mine. That makes me the girl they want to be for once. I'm on the top of the heap. A long way from a corporate slave, wouldn't you say?"

"Looks like you're way on top from down here," he said, referring to her height. Caden was tall; Siobhan was taller. Imanol sometimes called them The Two Towers when he was in one of his kinder moods.

"Maybe Shiny could turn Earth's gravity down just a bit for me."

"We won't stay here long," Caden said trivially. He sidestepped behind Siobhan, rubbed her shoulders, then headed for the door.

"I'll tell you what happens."

Siobhan nodded and waved. Caden walked out of the apartment and scanned the area for threats.

Here I am on the oldest home to Terrans, still looking around for danger like it's some nasty frontier planet. Terrans remain one of the greatest threats to Terrans.

Caden walked down the balcony that ran across the front of the building to a section of the platform that would take him down. The open elevator went down two floors, then stopped to pick up an attractive young woman.

Oh no.

She walked straight up to Caden.

"Mr. Lonrack... may I call you Caden? My name is Jenny. May I have a short interview?" she asked. At the same time, Caden's link got a request to accept payment of 10,000 ESC from her agency. He looked her up. She appeared to be a legitimate public information source, followed by... a billion Terrans in the Core Worlds.

Well, I do have a few expenses... and there are my parents.

He accepted the payment.

"Yeah, Caden is fine," he said.

"Caden! It's so wonderful to see you back on Earth! I speak for us all when I say, welcome back!"

Right. Speaking for a billion Core Worlders.

"Thanks Jenny."

"We're very curious, who do you work for now?" she asked.

"I work for Shiny on the PIT team." It felt strange to say that, knowing so many would hear his words. He felt like he had revealed a dark secret.

"Shiny? You call him that? You're on a first name basis with him?"

Caden shrugged. "Kind of. Our cultures are different, so I don't think it holds the meaning that you might assume it does. When we found him he wasn't an ambassador. He was just an alien we met in a Trilisk trap."

Jenny's jaw dropped. "Just an alien? A live alien! That you worked with to escape a Trilisk death trap! The adventures you must have had on the frontier, to say that so flippantly."

"I only meant he wasn't a formal ambassador as far as I knew. And it wasn't a death trap. It was probably a hotel for aliens, or a zoo, or a prison..."

The section of platform reached ground level, so Caden walked forward to find his cab. Jenny followed him. Caden was happy to see that there were not any other fans around. He wondered if Jenny had kept it secret so she could get her own private chat.

"Are you loyal to the UED?" she asked.

The question caught Caden off guard. "I've never been in the UED!"

"There were rumors of your connection to the UED before Ambassador Shiny brought his fleet in to oust the Trilisks," Jenny said.

I've met UED personnel on the frontier... no, don't say that.

"I've never thrown in with the UED. I've remained loyal to Earth. To the Terrans of Earth, that is, not the Trilisks who ruled here."

Jenny smiled widely. Caden walked up to his cab, a small blue electric cart that could only hold two people. He did not invite her aboard.

"Everyone wants to know what you've been up to out on the frontier."

"Exploration. Trying to find new allies for Earth. I think I should not divulge any details unless I have permission from my superiors."

Meaning Telisa, not Shiny.

"How is Miss Cutter?"

"Siobhan? She's doing well. Earth owes her a great debt. She was instrumental in overthrowing the Trilisks."

The interviewer chuckled politely.

"Well, I don't know about that. You certainly defend her loyally. She's been dubbed, 'the most hated woman on Earth', though she's hardly ever on Earth, so I don't know if that makes any sense. How does that make you feel?"

"I... wasn't aware. If anyone tries to harm her, it will be considered an attack on Ambassador Shiny, and the PIT team will react accordingly."

"You're widely considered the most desirable male by the GTW advisors."

"GTW? I'm sorry, I've been on a mission and I fell a bit behind. Does that still stand for—"

"Get Together Weekly, yes."

"I'm flattered, but I don't seek new relationships of... that kind, right now. I'm focused on my work."

"Forgive me, may I ask just one more question along this line? The women of Earth desperately want to know, are you in an exclusive arrangement with Ms. Cutter?"

Even as Caden hesitated he wondered if the hesitation was fatal. As soon as he realized he should answer quickly, he said firmly, "Yes."

"Ahhh, that's too bad," Jenny said and managed to sound sincere. "Would you be willing to be scanned and interviewed in depth for the creation of an accurate virtual profile? With demand as it is for personal Cadens in VRs, it would be very lucrative. There are already bids offered at over 1 million ESC."

"Very sorry, but not at this time," Caden said firmly.

"You must be on your way for your award ceremony at the Space Force surface headquarters. May I say I'm so glad to see you get the recognition you deserve, Mr. Lonrack!"

"Thanks Jenny. I'm sorry I have to leave now, or I'll be late."

"Thank you for the interview!" she called as Caden ducked into the cab and told the door to close after him.

Caden sat in silence for a minute, wondering about his new status on Earth. He had enjoyed being popular in school because of notable performance in many virtual competitions, but he had never sought fame across such a wide audience.

Do I need to hire a service to keep the crowds from me? Do I need to hide?

The cab drove in front of a reflective building. Caden idly caught sight of himself driving by. With a start he realized a large Vovokan sphere escorted him, just one or two meters above the cab. It kept perfect alignment with him, so rigidly that his brain told him it was attached to the vehicle though he could see no connection.

I guess Shiny's got it covered. And I'll head out on another mission soon anyway, then it won't matter.

The cab arrived at a security gate. It was the first level of defense of the Earthside Space Force headquarters in the northwest quadrant of Earth. The vehicle was scanned and allowed through. Caden's link got updates on his progress.

"The Space Force is honored to receive one of Earth's heroes, Caden Lonrack."

The conveyance continued down a simple but well-kept road. He saw the tops of buildings moving by over thick ceramic barriers.

The vehicle pulled up to a beautifully ornate gate. It did not look like Space Force standard fare.

"We're ready to receive you at the Honor Gate, Mr. Lonrack."

Honor Gate? Okay...

His link received a High Numbers Observation Warning, letting him know he was under realtime scrutiny by video feed viewers in excess of one hundred thousand. Caden released a nervous sigh. The attention had been so much more welcome when he was winning the Blood Glades.

Caden stepped carefully out of the vehicle and approached the gate.

HNOW: 140,000.

The gate opened. Caden walked forward. He saw a shadow and remembered the Vovokan sphere. He glanced upward. The sphere continued to rigidly move with him.

Is that thing going to come in?

Caden walked through the gate. His aerial bodyguard stopped in mid-air behind him. Ahead, four marines stood perfectly straight, PAWS strapped on their backs, guarding the Space Force checkpoint. Two laser domes were visible, overseeing the passage ahead.

Caden walked on. Ahead of him, one of the marines stepped forward.

"Welcome, Mr. Lonrack. Your escort is waiting just inside. If I may say so, it is an honor to meet you, Mr. Lonrack."

Caden felt odd. His old shame battled with this new attitude. Was the man sincere? *Could* he be sincere? Caden was happy that at least the man did not salute as some kind of additional honor; it would be ridiculous since Caden was not even an officer.

As Caden passed the checkpoint, four men flanked him and walked with him into a low building. His HNOW dropped, then went away entirely, as outside observation feeds were denied line of sight. Caden resisted the urge to look back for the drones that must be providing the feeds.

Caden and his escort all stepped onto a fast-moving conveyor that brought them into a building, then wound upwards to the second floor. They whisked through two corridors before stepping off next to a door. The platform before the door told Caden's link he stood in front of Admiral Sager's office.

The escorts stepped to either side of the door. One of them must have told it to open for Caden. Caden saw an old fashioned office inside, complete with a desk and bookcases that held what looked like real books.

Admiral Sager met Caden within. The escort did not follow him inside. The door closed behind him, leaving him alone with the Admiral. Caden noted again Sager's unusual amount of hair. The man had thin, pale lips and close set eyes.

Caden's link received several messages. One informed him he had been named a recipient of the Secretary of the Space Force Award for Valor. The next message declared he had received a monetary award of 20,000 ESC. Two subsequent messages offered him entrance to New Annapolis. Caden stood frozen, stunned.

"Mr. Lonrack. We would like to formally offer you a post in the Space Force. We've reviewed your preparatory training and your achievements. With a single year at New Annapolis to polish yourself, I feel sure you would be able to pass our tests and take your place as an officer. One on a fast track to the upper ranks, I might add."

"A single year? No one would respect an officer who—"

"On the contrary, Mr. Lonrack. You already have the respect of the Space Force. No one would complain. They understand the debt we owe you."

"We brought Ambassador Shiny into the system," Caden said. It felt strange to give the title to the Vovokan he had worked with. "The alien overlord who rules you all. We thought we brought him to save you, but instead we simply brought a new alien master to Earth."

"It turns out, casualties were very light. At the time of the Vovokan Revolution, as we call it, things were confused. We thought many had died. As it turns out, Ambassador Shiny minimized the death very effectively. A lot of hardware was damaged or destroyed, but he has since replaced that ten times over."

"And the deaths that did occur? No one blames me for those?"

"When the magnitude of what had happened to Terra became clear, we realized it was a small price to pay. The Space Force would have acted, if it could have, to remove the Trilisks itself, even at twice the price in blood we paid. You're a hero in everyone's eyes."

Caden felt a tide of emotions rise. He swallowed hard and tried to ride it out. He had not expected such a powerful reaction.

I guess I've gone from pariah to hero. I always wanted to be a Space Force hero, and it really happened, even though I never got to join up!

Caden told himself it was normal. He had released all the shame and tension that his actions had brought him. Now he had been vindicated at last.

I wonder if Siobhan had feelings like this when she killed that Trilisk who enslaved her family. She must have.

"Thank you, sir. I need to consider your offer carefully."

"Of course. Take your time," Admiral Sager said. The Admiral seemed to relax. Caden got the feeling the formalities were over.

"Where have you been, son? What do you do on the PIT team?"

Caden started to deflect the Admiral, then thought better of it.

"I shouldn't give away information, but I might be willing to trade..."

"I think we could come to an arrangement," the Admiral said amicably.

"I've been searching alien worlds for a race of advanced beings we call the Celarans. Shiny has sent us looking for them, or at least, their technologies. And we've come across a potential enemy of mankind, the ones who destroyed Shiny's homeworld."

"Ambassador Shiny has told us about that danger," Sager said. "He has been working with us to prepare the Space Force to defend our worlds from them."

Caden's eyebrows rose. "Does Shiny think we have a chance against them? Without Shiny's battleships, I mean."

"He says we can have an impact. He assures us our new weapons systems can harm them. He says he will stand with us."

Caden hesitated.

87

Will it come back to bite me if I throw doubt upon Shiny?

"Shiny's race does not understand loyalty," Caden said. "Just know, we may have to face them alone."

Sager listened to Caden carefully. He did not try to defend Shiny.

"What do you want to know about?" Sager asked.

"How has an alien come to lead Earth and the Space Force? How can you be okay with that, especially after the Trilisks? Surely you secretly plan to resist him."

A little too blatant, Caden. How will he react to that?

Sager smiled. "I'm willing to tell you the truth, but I don't know why you would believe me. Remember, if we were plotting against the Ambassador, you're a known ally of his, so I would be foolish to reveal anything to you."

Caden held up his hand. "Please start, then, with why the citizens of Earth seem to have accepted him."

"Well, he saved us from the Trilisks, to start."

"And then he took over from them."

"But he did it openly. And he has no orders for us. The Trilisks locked away the most influential citizens and controlled everything. They hurt our economies and cut into the citizens' VR quotas to produce space fleets for fighting their enemies."

Caden nodded. "I see most of that. You just said though, he was telling you to build weapons against the Destroyers."

"He merely provides insights into their weaknesses. Did you know, Caden, that the Destroyers were the race that took out the *Seeker*?"

Caden was taken aback. "No, I had no idea."

"Well, we're glad to have his advice. And we have the resources we need to maintain our new fleet. So for now at least, we work with him."

Caden nodded. "I'm hoping we can find Celarans. There are a few clues that they're friendly. Though we search for Shiny, we'll represent Terrans if we encounter living Celarans."

"If you go looking for them, please do tell me what you find," Sager said. "We'd like to send a formal diplomatic party if we can locate these Celarans."

"I promise I'll do my best," Caden said. "I have a web of loyalties to navigate, but I always want to do what's best for Terrans everywhere."

"I have other work I have to get to," Sager said. "Consider our offer. It's genuine."

Sager offered Caden his hand. It was a rare gesture that made Caden feel honored. Caden shook it. Then the Admiral dismissed him. Caden's mind reeled with recent events and he wanted to find someplace private to think things over.

I need to talk to Siobhan and Telisa.

Caden escaped the headquarters as quickly as he could. He got another HNOW, but it was dramatically smaller than before. The fickle public must have moved on.

Once alone in a taxi vehicle, Caden exhaled. That had been heavy.

"Siobhan?" he sent on a private channel.

"Caden. I heard you made it," her voice came back over the link.

"Yes. They offered me entrance to New Annapolis. I deflected questions about it. I feel a lot of pressure."

"Don't worry about what the Earthers want; it's them who owe *you*, remember? Do what you want."

Caden nodded. "I used to want to be a Space Force officer more than anything else, but I've learned so much. I want to stay on the PIT team now."

Siobhan smiled. "So do I."

Michael McCloskey

Chapter 15

The circular portal dared Imanol to proceed. He felt a familiar weight of commitment.

I've come this far, can I really turn back now?

He took a single step forward.

Of course you could turn back now, you idiot.

Imanol thought about handing the sphere back to Telisa and telling her he did not find out if the Trilisk AI was here. It would be so much easier to avoid all of this and go back.

He shook his head and walked through the black zone. He emerged on the other side in a black tunnel with smooth walls. Rather than providing a flat path to walk on, the entire passage was perfectly round. Imanol remembered it: the Trilisk catacombs. On this side of the blackfield, he saw two banks of small, reddish blocks attached to the gray metal of the disk that he had stepped through.

Vovokan cybernetics.

Imanol's link brought up his map from the last time he had visited the tunnels. If he compared the tunnels he saw now to his old map, he figured he would be able to orient himself quickly. The stealth suit also had an inertial navigation system that would let him know his location. That could be matched up to the old map, where at least he knew the exact location of the entrance before he had entered the tunnels.

He wondered for a moment if Shiny could have changed the layout. At first, he dismissed the idea; the Trilisk materials were so durable as to be almost permanent, even in the face of those determined to damage them. Then, he remembered the AIs. Surely Shiny could have prayed for the tunnels to reconfigure any way he wanted.

Imanol walked down the black tunnel. As the glow from the Vovokan devices faded behind him, his eyes adjusted to a low level light with no apparent source. He started to check to see if he cast a shadow, then realized with the cloaking device active, he could not see his shadow anyway. He decided the light must emerge evenly from the entire surface of the tunnel.

Shouldn't the walls glow if they all emit light evenly? I can see but they don't glow. He shrugged. *Trilisks.*

The place seemed deserted, but he did not see any dust anywhere along the inside surface. He dropped to wipe the floor with a hand as he went. He did not feel anything except the smooth surface. That's how the Trilisks made things: incredibly durable, self-cleaning, and perfect down to the last molecule. He decided he could not make any conclusion about how often the tunnel was being used.

The tunnel branched once, so Imanol walked left, then it branched again. He found a match on his old map for the branchings.

I think I know where I am. So, I guess there is really only one place to go.

If he was right, the temple was in a different direction. Imanol altered course to find the temple. He walked calmly but quickly. By his old map, he had covered most of a long stretch of tunnel when he saw something ahead. His mind first resolved it as the end of the tunnel, then with a shock, he understood it was a sphere in the tunnel—headed straight for him. Despite his body's reaction to a dump of adrenaline, he remained mentally calm. It could hardly be going any other direction in the tunnel, so it might not be targeting him at all. He dropped prone on the right side of the curved floor. He estimated there would be room for it to pass by without touching him.

The sphere came closer. It looked large coming down the center of the space, though Imanol thought that perhaps two such machines might just be able to squeeze by each other in the tunnels.

Vovokan machines are hard to judge. If everything is a bloody sphere, how can you tell what the stupid thing does?

Instinctual fear rose in Imanol. His forced calm started to crack. It was impossible to watch the silent, sinister sphere approach and not feel dread. He stared down at the floor ahead of him, mastering himself and staying perfectly still. If it was a war machine, he would be no match for its speed and power at this range.

The sphere floated overhead and continued on its path. Imanol remained in that position for a minute after it left, allowing his heart to slow.

Okay, it's fine. I should have more faith in the stealth sphere. It got me through the blackfield checkpoint, it'll get me through the rest of this.

The old route proved accurate. He saw a light grow ahead into the entrance to a huge chamber. This time, instead of an ancient temple, Imanol saw a vast cavern, shaped with natural curves like a real cave, except larger than any Imanol had ever seen. At the center of the open space sat a perfectly square, white building which extended from floor to ceiling. Some of its walls were transparent, showing Imanol glimpses of simple white rooms within. He saw a patch of Vovokan circuitry in one. Another held a Trilisk column.

So that's it, then. No more temple. He modernized it. Vovokans are weird. Why not just use this whole space? He makes it look like a natural cave. Just for looks?

Imanol felt relief. As irrational as it was, he felt relief that he would not have to walk through that place again. He approached the white building and found a large circular door where the sandy floor met the white walls. He imagined to be the right size for Shiny... or that Trilisk.

He stopped in front of the door to look around. There were no footprints in the sand, but he knew the sand was recycled to carry away any garbage or waste. If no one moved through here but a select few, how could he get through the door undetected?

I could wait here. Who knows how long? I have a few of Cilreth's Vovokan hacks to try. She said they were like what a Vovokan child might throw together.

Imanol told one of his attendant spheres to detach from him and move through the door. It emerged from his stealth zone, into full sight, to hover in front of the door. The portal opened.

Imanol slowed its passage through the door so he could follow. Once through, the door closed and he retrieved the attendant.

So much for being completely undetectable.

The room beyond held only a bank of Vovokan machinery. It was a collection of tubes and glowing parts, like a kid's project blox creation, that came as high as his hip. Imanol did not touch or investigate; instead, he walked through another circular opening.

The connecting room was even bigger and brighter, with white walls.

There in the center of the room, Imanol saw a Trilisk. He froze for a moment before he realized it was not free to move. The creature was placed onto a column or saddle that fit its odd shape perfectly. The three legs dangled around the perimeter. With a shudder, he remembered the three-tusked maw on its underside, hidden by the column. One of its grotesque eyes faced him, so large it made Imanol think again of the creature as a giant face with legs and arms.

Blood and souls...

Wires and tubes clustered around the column and entered the Trilisk from all angles. Several went into the slit underneath the eye that faced him. Imanol realized he had his projectile pistol out and aimed at the thing. He lowered his weapon and walked very slowly along the outside wall, giving the Trilisk a wide berth. His perspective shifted until he could see two of its three 'faces' in equal proportions. He shuddered again. That made it look *more* like a giant face, not less, because now he could see two eyes.

Get a hold of yourself, man. What is it about this damn Trilisk that scares me so much? Ugly is one thing, but it makes me shake.

Imanol looked down to double check he was still invisible. The creature did not react to his presence. It simply stared off into space as if experiencing a VR. It occurred to him that he could not trust his instincts when it came to such a creature. For all he knew, this is exactly how it behaved just before attacking.

He steeled himself and stepped closer. He could see tiny ridges on its dark rubbery surface. He remembered the awful strength of the Trilisk he had encountered. He wondered if this was the same one.

Blood and souls, should I hate it or feel sorry for it?

Imanol realized the answer was the same either way: kill it. But he had not accomplished his main goal of finding the AI. Surely if he assassinated this Trilisk, the Vovokan security would be alerted. Then he might not be able to escape.

It could make a useful distraction.

Imanol checked to make sure he had not missed any doors behind him. He wanted to choose a spot that might not be observed. He set one of this grenades for detonation in three hours and let it roll quietly over to the base of the pillar. He squatted to check its position. From down low, it looked painfully obvious, but the equipment protruded above it, making it unlikely to spot from above.

Imanol finally felt a sense of achievement. At least now, maybe his visit would prove productive. He turned back and left the room the way he had come. His attendant made the door open once more so he could exit.

Within the adjacent chamber, Imanol stopped to think.

Go back now? I haven't found it. I need to check the rest of the complex.

Imanol let the attendant move through the rest of the strange white building while he watched its feed. He did not see anything as interesting as the Trilisk in the rest of the rooms, so he told the attendant to emerge from the building so he could follow it out.

Imanol eyed the tunnel he had arrived from, but he forced himself to walk around the special enclosure and choose another tunnel. He headed into the tunnel, moving quickly; he was on the clock now. Normally he might have been able to send a grenade a detonation command, but he figured the Trilisk tunnels might well block such signals.

The new tunnel soon opened into a black hexagonal room. Tunnels exited from three of the six sides. Like the tunnels, light enabled him to see everything even though he could not spot lone sources of illumination.

A spinning sphere floated in the center of the room. Small rods protruded radially all over its surface, lit by green lasers from several points nearby. The floor below it looked like black glass with a million tiny dimples melted into it. A flat path ran a circle around the center, providing access to the other exits without having to cross the center.

Telisa had once described the Trilisk device to him as a sphere with eerie floating rods revolving around and merging into it. When he asked for specifics, she just said "you'll know it when you see it."

As Imanol watched, some of the rods slid across its surface. Others slipped into the sphere and disappeared.

Okay, that's it. It's here. It looks... healthy. Shiny probably fixed it with the other AI, or gave it the power it needed, or whatever. We know where it is, and how to get it if we wanted to make a grab for it.

The thought of taking it right now crossed his mind. He quashed it. The PIT team was not ready to exploit such a bold opportunity right now. Maybe if they came up with a coordinated plan.

When we do, I might have to come back. Sigh. Or could I give the layout to someone else and let them do it? Problem for another time.

Imanol turned away from the Trilisk artifact and backtracked. He went out the tunnel he had arrived through. He now saw the end of this ordeal. He had found out that Shiny did have the AI, it had been kept here, and Imanol got the added bonus of killing off the Trilisk.

Mission accomplished.

Imanol kept walking. As his doubts grew, his pace increased.

What will Shiny do when it dies? Would he know who did it? With the PIT team back in-system, he'll suspect Telisa.

He considered pulling the grenade on his way back out. Before he could decide, he saw an anomaly ahead. It was another spherical machine, headed down the tunnel toward him.

Imanol went prone again. He took a deep breath and held it. The same eerie feeling haunted him as he watched the sphere draw ever closer.

Just ride it out...

The sphere stopped above him.

Blood and souls.

The stealth sphere sent Imanol's link a simple failure message: "Stealth mode failure due to lack of power." That did not sound right to Imanol. The alien stealth device had not been perfectly interfaced with Terran link protocols, though. The actual problem might be something different, but at this point it did not matter: Imanol had been detected.

Maybe the AI saw me and disabled it? Or maybe the sphere expends a lot more power to hide in a place like this?

Imanol rolled away. The sphere did not move. He pushed himself back onto his feet and ran back the way he had come. He had his link mark the path he had taken to arrive just to be sure.

What's it doing?

One glance back told him the sphere had started to move after him.

It can move faster than that. Why so slow? Oh. Because I'm going the way it wants me to.

He continued. He had no choice. The tunnel did not branch for another hundred meters. He looked back again and saw the sphere had closed the distance.

Is this it?

The huge sphere sent a bolt of energy into Imanol. His body convulsed and collapsed onto the black Trilisk floor.

Imanol's limbs twitched. He struggled to move without success. He faded in and out of consciousness.

Something picked him up from the floor.

Later, he was vaguely aware of the sphere nearby.

His confusion slowly cleared. Had he been moving? He stared at the perfect section of the tunnel above and could not tell. Then, a change in the geometry above showed him they were moving. The ceiling above became a flat black surface instead of the curved top of a cylindrical tunnel.

He floated back down to the floor. Imanol was able to roll over. His limbs started to respond to his commands at last. A clacking sound grew in his ears. He immediately classified it: the sound of many Vovokan feet hitting a ceramic floor. Shiny was coming.

Imanol caught sight of mottled gold. His vision cleared a bit, resolving until he saw a small forest of golden trunks with sharp ends. His limbs flinched, then he found he could control his body again.

"Well, if it isn't the Shining One," Imanol grumbled, cautiously tilting his head to look at Shiny. The alien shocked him again with its complex appearance. He saw dozens of golden legs and a long, almost serpentine body. One end of the alien hovered a meter from his head. It was the smooth, featureless end with the tiny clusters of light sensors hanging beneath that looked like golden enoki with tiny little crab eyes. Imanol decided Shiny's golden coloration really saved his appearance for Terrans. If the alien had been mottled gray or green, he would be a real terror.

"You are Imanol." The answer came to Imanol's link.

"How did you see me? I thought the sphere was advanced enough to fool the mass sensors."

"This area high security. Shiny finds, notices, detects trace molecules from passage, footsteps, path of Imanol. Then attendant, servant, sight spheres appear from cloaked regions, zones, areas."

"What are you doing here?"

"Shiny away, absent, distant. Imanol speaks with projected, transmitted, illusory Shiny only."

Can it be true? I heard his feet hitting the floor. Good illusion, I guess.

"Oh. Got it. So you've harnessed Earth's Trilisk machine."

"Correct, affirmative, verified."

"That's how you control the Terrans, isn't it? You have them under mind control of some kind," said Imanol.

"Incorrect, negative, false. Shiny pleases Terran citizens."

Imanol did not believe the alien.

"When I was down here before, I saw a Trilisk. Is it the same one down this corridor?"

Imanol found himself hoping Shiny would reply in the negative. He wanted that thing to be a Trilisk pet, something evolved on the same planet as the Trilisks that shared the trinary structure of the ancient race, anything he could dismiss and laugh off as a good scare.

"Correct, affirmative, verified."

"What are you doing to it?" he asked.

Could that thing have taken over Shiny?

"Trilisk is trapped, incarcerated, imprisoned. Shiny studies alien."

Blood and souls, surely he's gone too far?

"Aren't you worried about it taking over your AIs? Isn't it dangerous?"

"Trilisk is compromised, reduced, damaged. It is insane, unstable, broken. Trilisk left to guard outpost, complex, headquarters very long ago. Trilisk enemies attacked, causing extensive damage, destruction, impairment. This one survived. Events, time, circumstances destroyed Trilisk reason, mind, consciousness."

"And the Trilisk AI? It let this happen?"

"Outpost damaged, dysfunctional, broken. Shiny uses other AI to repair, restore, refurbish."

What else should I ask? Telisa should know all this.

"But you didn't tell the AI to restore the Trilisk."

"Shiny deems mentioned course of action reckless, unwise, inadvisable."

"I agree. Have you spoken with Telisa? Did you reach a new agreement?"

"Negotiations continue."

That news was better than Imanol had expected. He decided to stop probing and start begging.

"I apologize for the intrusion. I was just curious. Can I leave? Telisa wants me to head back soon."

"Soon, quickly, imminently," Shiny responded. "First, Imanol subject to modification, alteration, enhancement."

Blood and souls.

"Uhm. Modification?"

"Shiny requires new function, usage, utility from Imanol. Done, complete, finished."

"I didn't feel anything—"

Imanol blinked. He found himself back at the tunnel entrance, facing the dock. The stealth sphere told him he was once again invisible.

What was I just thinking about? I have a bad feeling about this.

Michael McCloskey

Chapter 16

Cilreth walked into a specialized software demo shop in Brazil. She supposed the business going on there was a cover, though it probably generated revenue. People walked back and forth inside a three story set of office suites with a wide open atrium at the center that cut up through all three floors. Cilreth quickly summed up the activity as pairings between representatives and customers; the incarnate offices probably helped to encourage illicit, and therefore very profitable, transactions.

Of the people working at *Código Vermelho,* Cilreth had found nine employees that could be Marcant or a close partner.

Cilreth caught the eye of a young woman with black hair in a checkered red outfit. Her hair was longer in front than the back, so it sheltered her eyes. The pattern on her clothes changed every few seconds. Cilreth smiled. No doubt it changed according to some obscure algorithm the girl appreciated.

"What's your emergency?" the girl asked in English. She did not smile, but she at least feigned interest effectively.

"I'm here for Marcant. And don't bother to tell me I'm in the wrong place. I'm well beyond that."

"An old lady like you thinks she can find Marcant? That's funny," said a male voice.

Cilreth turned and saw the source: an adolescent boy with bright blond hair. He leaned his skinny body against a nearby counter and stared at Cilreth. She noticed his eyes follow her form down her torso.

"I got this far, didn't I?" Cilreth challenged. "I don't really need your purple paste."

"What's your nick?"

"1154688075."

"Wow, a real grabber," the blond kid said sarcastically. But the girl with short hair and a pale face did not smile.

"That wasn't you," the girl challenged back, head held level so that her bangs still hid her eyes.

"Still is me," Cilreth said. Some ire bled into her voice.

What do these idiots have to do with Marcant?

"Why do you want to talk to Marcant?" asked the girl.

The blond kid looked at the girl in irritation, but he did not interrupt.

"I have a job offer."

The kid scoffed. Cilreth took a deep breath and tried again.

"Tell him or her or it I have a legit job offer. A chance to work on real Vovokan hardware."

"*Vovokan?*" the kid asked. "You work for Shiny? Shiny wants to hire Marcant?"

The girl flashed a look of anger at the kid.

"Shut your mouth," the girl told him. She finally pushed her hair off her face. Green glowing eyes took their first direct look at Cilreth. Then she pointed across the store. "Go," she told the kid. The boy left.

"Come over here," the girl said. Cilreth followed her to the nearest wall, made of a transparent material. They passed through a clear door and into a partial VR booth of about 100 cubic meters. A headset sat on the floor. Cilreth realized it had been a long time since she had used anything like it. Telisa swore by them, since pseudo VR exercised the body. Cilreth just took toning pills and stayed lazy.

The girl turned to Cilreth and continued talking.

"You *do* work for Shiny," she said.

"I'm not his biggest fan right now," Cilreth said. "But yes, Shiny is our direct source of Vovokan hardware and I know how to use Vovokan systems. I can spill it all to Marcant, if he comes to work with the PIT team."

It felt strange for Cilreth to talk about PIT with a stranger. It still had not sunk in that the team had become famous because of their connection to Shiny.

"I've never seen a more obvious trap in all my life. Which is strange, because Shiny's smart. Very smart."

"I expected some amount of suspicion. Look, the PIT team comes in contact with alien stuff, not just Vovokan. Can you think of anyone more qualified than Marcant to look into it? If Marcant really exists."

"Why did you come here looking for him?"

"Research," Cilreth said.

"There's nothing publicly available that links Marcant to this place, or to me."

"I didn't say I was researching public information," Cilreth said.

"Shiny's never sent goons here before," she said.

"You guys can't break Shiny. His whole raced lived to screw each other over. His security is beyond ours."

"So?"

"So he doesn't need to send goons. He knows even Marcant isn't a threat."

"You have a bounty on your head," she said.

What? Marcant put a bounty on me for looking for him?

The girl stared over her shoulder. Cilreth stepped forward and to one side, not wanting to take her eyes off the girl. She dared a look.

Two men in rugged clothing were making their way through the establishment toward them.

"You must have stolen a lot of drugs from those nice people," the girl said, taking a step away from Cilreth.

Cilreth had no idea what she was talking about. She released three attendant spheres from her waist pack and pulled her combo laser/stunner pistol off her hip. One attendant told her the wall behind her was not very substantial. She could see the support beams ran up from floor to ceiling only on the corners of the VR cubicle.

The girl stared in alarm at the spheres. Cilreth ignored her.

Cilreth sent an attendant through the wall. No one was on the other side.

"I'll be back," Cilreth said, then she rammed through the wall. Its substance cracked under her impact and fell away in hand-sized chunks.

The attendant she had left behind told her one of the men had run into the booth. Cilreth turned and faced the hole. Her heart slammed in her chest, but she knew she had to bloody a nose to slow down her pursuers.

She stepped aside to avoid being spotted, then aimed her pistol back at the hole. She selected the stun functionality. The weapon told her it would have to log her shots to function in the lounge.

Cthulhu's balls, we didn't hack this weapon yet. Out on the frontier we get lazy about these things.

A tall, dark skinned man thrust through the opening, weapon in hand. Cilreth had only an instant to size him up: the man looked determined and aggressive.

"Log this," Cilreth said, firing the weapon in the face of the man. He fell back out of sight. The weapon verified the target had been rendered unconscious.

She turned and ran through the back room. It held a dizzying array of boxes and pseudo VR exercise machines. Cilreth found it odd for a custom software shop, but she wasted no time puzzling it over.

I wonder if they have someone on the back entrance.

Cilreth sent one attendant to scout a possible exit in the back. She went through a doorway which led into the other side of store, crouching low to keep her head obscured by the flat advertisement anchor screens and the people standing around VR chairs and mixed VR towers.

The other man was easy to spot. He was headed right toward the service door she had emerged from. She fired her stunner at him but he ducked away at the same time.

Cilreth dove down an aisle of demo stations to avoid counterfire. Four people stood in partial VR stations, exercising their bodies while experiencing artificial input into their brains. They had no idea anything dangerous was happening around them.

One attendant spotted her adversary and tailed him. A second one showed her a suspicious car out front with more men waiting inside. The last attendant showed an unguarded back alley.

Cilreth used the feed of the man hunting her in the store to double back the way she had come without being seen. The attendant fed her the exit route while she watched the other enemy search for her. She fled through the back door and sprinted away, using the debris in the alleyway to cover her escape.

Cilreth felt proud of herself.

I did it! I smoothly integrated off-retina input in a combat situation and used it to my advantage.

A couple of years ago she would have laughed at the idea of being so happy with such a thing. Now, she could appreciate the complexity of what she had done. She lacked the grace of Telisa and the tactical precision of Caden, but it was a solid job. Cilreth hurried away from the shop, losing herself in a crowd of android work bodies and incarnate tourists. Five minutes later, she contacted Telisa and gave her a report.

"I'm making progress. I found someone who knows him, and she'll send him a message," she said.

Telisa answered after a few seconds. "How will you intercept the message? Or do you just track it?"

"She could send a carrier pigeon for all I know. I'll figure something out."

Cilreth considered telling Telisa about her other drug problem, but she decided against it.

"Keep me up to date," Telisa said.

"What did Shiny say about Magnus?"

"Well he didn't say no."

"Shiny never speaks that plainly."

"I mean, even allowing for his way of talking, he didn't say no."

"So far so good? I may need you later."

"Yep. What do you think you'll need?"

"Well, Marcant's next level of security may be more... physical."

"Ah. I can probably help you with that."

"Exactly what I had hoped you might say."

***

Cilreth continued her research into Marcant from the relative safety of a hotel room. She linked into Vovokan resources in order to both obscure and empower her search. She checked on the progress of her ongoing investigation. A set of results had been waiting for her, describing Marcant's past exploits and his particular resources and talents. She had not yet reviewed the results since her priority had been on identifying and finding him.

The profile was stereotypical: that of a young, bright kid prone to crime, who honed his skills and eventually turned from selfish acts to selfless ones. Marcant used his amazing skills to fight the oppressive government and megacorporations at every turn. He had avoided Core World Security his entire career. He had never been caught. As she absorbed the material, it started to feel wrong to Cilreth. She read for another few minutes until she became sure about it.

This is too smooth, too epic. It's fabricated. Marcant has put this out to obscure the truth.

Cilreth opened her eyes and crossed her arms. How could she find out more? She thought of the two young people in the store. They knew about Marcant. Word of mouth. Maybe not passed incarnate, but nevertheless passed in conversation, not online investigations.

Time to shift methods.

Cilreth went back off-retina and opened some new viewpanes. She dusted off some of her old programs which were designed to gather information. The programs went online and pretended to be kids asking questions about things, pestering the older kids. What the older kids heard on the street, they told their siblings about; then the information filtered down to younger kids. The information was always distorted, but it could be useful.

This time, she used the social network model she had created to help find Marcant, and lent more weight to sources closer to him on the graph. Information *had to be* flowing outwards from those in the know to the lesser ranked and skilled followers who wanted to learn from them.

Cilreth set the new experiment in motion. Results started coming back within minutes. She checked a few conversations just to make sure things were working. It did not have much so far. That was to be expected. The system would rank results as they came in so she could look at the top clues whenever she liked.

She saw one conversation where Marcant was described as being "augmented". She supposed that pointed toward him being a Terran with cybernetic or genetic changes for higher intelligence.

The next flagged conversation looked useful:

"What's his thing? He seems like quite the cult of personality around here."

"Augmented human intelligence."

"Better link? Genetics? What?"

"He's fully integrated with two AIs. They work symbiotically. You know, the whole greater than the sum of its parts."

Cilreth considered that. It sounded about as solid as anything could get using this method. She told her fleet to start conversations to verify the rumor. Within another hour, it had solidified. True or not, it was what the scientists, engineers, and hackers in Marcant's network believed: Marcant had a special rapport with AIs, ones he had written himself, and he had integrated his mind with them to a degree more extreme than anyone had done before.

Totally illegal. Well, I guess that government isn't here anymore.

Cilreth had heard of soldiers the Space Force had integrated with AIs to improve battle performance, both on the battlefield and in space operations. This sounded a lot like that, though if the stories were to be believed, Marcant had cooked it up himself.

This guy could be useful to the team. Sounds like just what I want... but how am I going to find him?

Chapter 17

"We have a new problem," Adair said.

Marcant hated it when Adair said such things. It always went the same from this point: Marcant would attempt to dismiss it, and Adair would convince him otherwise. Then Achaius would suggest an aggressive solution and the argument would shift toward the future.

"Tell me," Marcant said.

"Someone from the PIT team is after you," Adair said. Marcant's breath stopped. The feeling of anxiety grew from his gut. "That IS a problem," he said.

How bad is it when I agree with Adair from the beginning?

"Your vitals speak for you," Adair said.

"I wasn't expecting something so concrete. Usually you tell me we have to worry about something nebulous a month in the future."

"Well this Cilreth is days away," Adair said. "She walked into the Jaguar shop this afternoon and made it clear she knows you're connected. She said she wanted to offer you a job."

Marcant had heard enough to know Cilreth was the name of a PIT member. He also knew that Adair and Achaius would have more details for him.

"What do we know about Cilreth?" Marcant asked.

"She was a tracker, at least she was before joining their team," Achaius said. "Recently, she's gotten into some trouble with a large illegal drug distributor. She had a tangle with them in the Jaguar, in fact."

"The results?"

"She held her own in a strategic retreat. Good training, but not a talent of hers, I'd say," Achaius said.

Marcant knew Achaius had very high standards when it came to tactical actions. If the AI core said she had good training, then she would be at least 95th percentile.

"What's a druggie doing on the PIT team?" Marcant asked.

"Not really a druggie, just a twitch addict," Adair said. "But truly, she killed a house full of people to get a bunch of twitch. Doesn't sound like the angels the media says are in PIT, does it?"

"This is an elite strike team created by the alien Shiny," Achaius said. "Everyone likes him, but he has machinations going on behind the scenes. He could be worse than the Trilisks."

"He rules in the open. That seems better to me," Marcant said, but his voice was laced with doubt.

"You haven't asked the real question," Adair prompted.

"I know. Is Cilreth looking for me because of our cell copy fiasco?" Marcant asked as prompted.

"And?"

"And why send a lone Terran instead of a collection of flying death spheres," Marcant finished.

"I say, no coincidence," Achaius said.

Marcant nodded. "So Shiny knows who and what, but not where? So she comes looking, because a Terran can snoop information out that a bunch of force might not get?"

"He can take people in by force and get anything he needs out of them," Adair said. "He has chosen not to use force. He has chosen to be nice."

Why? Could she be telling the truth?

"Adair. We need to find out every single scrap of—"

"Information about the PIT team," Adair finished for him. "I'm so far ahead of you jelly-brain, let me tell you. So far that you—"

"Okay then pal, bring me up to threshold voltage and let the info flow."

"We've identified nine individuals that are certainly part of the team, or have been part of the team. A few more are suspected at various levels," Adair began. "First, the commonalities. The team travels. In every public appearance they have shown themselves to be fit. Their movements indicate a combination of real physical and virtual training. Whenever possible they are armed and armored in the manner of frontier explorers at least, if not outright mercenaries."

"To the specifics then," Marcant said. "Telisa. She started all this?"

"Actually she's the fourth known member," Adair said. "The first one is Jack Parker himself, founder. An artifact smuggler."

"Let me guess. The company was never really about map making, touring, or private scouting. It was about smuggling from the beginning," Marcant said.

"Exactly," Adair said. "The first ship went out several times with Parker and his pilot, Thomas Haist, and an ex-Space Force man, Magnus Garrison."

"Capable and self-motivated people. Independent. Not afraid to break the law," Marcant summarized.

"Sounds like someone else I know," Achaius said. Marcant ignored him.

"This Magnus. Was he high-ranking?"

"No, not at all," Adair said. "He's intelligent and as far as we know, skilled. But he was never an influence powerhouse in the Space Force. I see the roots of the vigorous PIT training regimen in him. It mirrors that of the Space Force. Less rotted by the indulgences of virtual reality, yet incorporating virtual exercises for learning."

"So Telisa comes in next?"

"Yes. A student of xenoarchaeology," Adair continued. "We have more records on her than anyone else. Telisa starts out as one of the good-at-everything-great-at-nothing kids typical of a generation fifty years past the launch of manufactured genes. She gets her elementary education with a ten-year download package for all the math and language basics. She's smart, charismatic, athletic, and as it turns out, determined."

"Rare. How does she get onto PIT?" asked Marcant.

"PIT picked her up, presumably because of her expertise and interest in alien artifacts. Soon thereafter I believe they actually met Shiny out past the frontier."

"So they meet a live alien, and they fall in together. I wonder what was in it for Ambassador Shiny?"

"That isn't clear. And it gets less clear from there," Adair said. "Parker and Haist disappear after Telisa's first trip. They have never been seen since. The PIT headquarters used android lookalikes of them for a while, probably covering for their disappearance. We don't know if they operate from the frontier or if something happened to them, but their relatives on Earth and other Core Worlds act as if they believe Parker and Haist are dead. Telisa's father is infamously involved in a covered up encounter with aliens in his command of the scout ship *Seeker*. A ship later destroyed by aliens... but Relachik does not share its fate. Instead he disappears with a team of his own, including Cilreth Sanders, known to be a current member of the team."

"This could all have started with her father. Maybe he met Ambassador Shiny on a Space Force mission no one knows about," Marcant said. "The rest could be orchestrated."

"Pure speculation, but possible," Adair said. "Cilreth is the one after you now. She's made scary fast progress on this, jelly brain. This is going to come to a head sooner than later."

"Tell me more about Cilreth."

"A tracker and twitch addict as mentioned. Smart enough, but pre-PIT team, nothing special really."

"Tracker and bounty hunter?" asked Marcant.

"No, just the people finding part, not the physical part."

"Then she's sticking to her specialty; she's finding me. But once found, she's not the death squad. Maybe it's not so bad," Marcant said. "Who else do we know about? Caden Lonrack, obviously. The super popular Blood Glades champ turned Space Force hero."

"That's right. I think the PIT team needed some more muscle," Achaius said. "Caden would be combat capable for a Terran."

"Maybe she finds me and he kills me. But why not use robots? Terrans aren't muscle anymore. Robots are."

"True enough, but maybe the robots were too difficult to handle in the Trilisk age," Achaius said.

"Another theory: Shiny wants to keep his hands clean of this," Adair said.

Marcant sat in silence for a moment. "And the other PIT members?"

"Siobhan Cutter is more than simply the reported 'most envied woman on Earth'. She's a frontier automation specialist. Once again, a great candidate for a team like PIT, at least, if the PIT team does what we think it does. She's tall, from a lower grav world. She had a beef with one of the Trilisks posing as a corporate leader."

My view of PIT is polluted by hype. There's more going on here, but no one knows what.

"What do we think PIT does now? Can we verify anything?"

"They work with Shiny. They travel to the frontier and beyond. They have sold alien artifacts to Core World buyers. They've killed Trilisks. This we know for sure. There are rumors of UED contacts. That may be simply a piece of the campaign against the Trilisks."

"Who else?"

"Jason Yang: A sharp business mind who ran the PIT cover company. He seems to have moved up and taken a more active role. He's selling the cover company right now."

"Yes, it's useless. Everyone knows about it. Are there more?"

"Suspected members: Imanol McCollum, Maxsym Kirilenko, Leonard Relachik, Arlin Donovan."

"Anything on them?" asked Marcant.

"McCollum is a private investigator, borderline mercenary, competent, but not successful before joining the team. Kirilenko is a top notch xenobiologist. No mystery there. Relachik, of course, is Telisa's father. Donovan worked security on the frontier, possibly turned merc. These four are off the radar at the moment. We don't know where they are."

"I wonder if the team always travels together on the frontier, or if some of them are still out there while these others visit Earth," Marcant said. "That's it?"

"We have one more glimpse. It's very interesting and comes from the Space Force," Achaius said.

"The Space Force gave up this tidbit voluntarily?"

"No, not so much. More of the results of a deep dig. I learned that the Space Force briefly put a spy into the PIT team. He was rooted out almost immediately. But he was released alive."

"That surprises me, given how many of these people have just disappeared."

"Maybe it was compassion, or maybe it was a deal. But when debriefed, the spy reported the presence of one Jamie Arakaki of the UED."

Marcant shook his head again. "The UED connection."

"Actually almost no one knows about *this* UED connection. The one that people speak of in conspiracies is that supposedly Telisa Relachik negotiated with the UED to have them help control Earth in the wake of the Trilisk removal. The rumor is traced back to some high sources in the UED, but we don't know if the idea was manufactured by them to help them out in case they made a power grab."

"They must have been thinking about it, in the wake of Ambassador Shiny's takeover," Marcant said.

"I don't see why they needed the UED," Achaius said. "Shiny's ships were more than up to the task of neutralizing the UNSF. They may have wanted help going after the Trilisks in the system. I'm not satisfied with that answer, though."

"I think Arakaki was simply recruited like the others," Adair said. "I can't explain the other rumors about the UED. It's possible Arakaki was a spy for the UED on the team, or the other way around. She may have tipped off the UED about the attack on Earth. The UED might have been readying for an attack of their own, but backed down once they saw how outclassed they were."

"I assume that there could be more team members."

"There probably are more we don't know about," Adair agreed.

Marcant was quiet for a minute, thoughts churning in his head.

"They may want to kill me, or they could really want to recruit me as she claims," he said. "If they do want to offer me a job, what happens if I say no?"

"Don't take the risk. Don't let them get to you," Adair said.

"Don't say no. Say yes. We can work from there, on the inside," Achaius said.

"If they're sounding me out, it needs to be convincing. I have to be want they want," Marcant said. "So I should fit their profile if I can. I should hate Trilisks, apparently. I should want to work for Shiny. Be an explorer."

"My confidence is low," Adair said. "You haven't left this place in months."

"I could be an explorer," Marcant said defensively, but his thoughts were different.

Damn. He's right. I'm the opposite of an explorer.

Michael McCloskey

Chapter 18

Jason rode along the west side 30th story pedestrian causeway in Manhattan, surrounded by strangers. He wore frontier clothing and gave his hair a 24 hour tint for a quick disguise. Before his arrival, he had turned off his location broadcast as well as flipped off permission for tracking by automatic public sensor feed recognition. No doubt Core World Security still knew exactly where he was, but strangers and news agencies were forbidden from tracking him on these settings.

He had come to Manhattan to close out the last of his equipment caches and try to meet with CWS. Some of the stations they had set up to monitor Trilisks had been cleaned up by various authorities. The ones left here were intact and still drawing funds for no benefit. As he moved along the wide pedestrian conveyor, he wondered if CWS had broken in and examined their equipment. He decided they must have.

They should like me. The equipment and data I left behind shows I really was after the Trilisks and not anything else.

In his musings, Jason was only peripherally aware of a person standing near him on his right. Then she spoke to him.

"Jason Yang?"

Jason looked up and stared. She had beautiful eyes and shiny black hair. Suddenly he recognized her.

"You! I saw you in Stark's," he stammered.

"Yes. Imagine how shocked I was when I found out you were telling me the truth about saving the world! I have to admit I didn't believe you at the time."

Jason smiled at her and struggled for words. "So we meet again. Seems unlikely."

Warning bells within Jason's head struggled to be heard over her hypnotic beauty.

"It's no coincidence," she said. "I found you."

She found me? Too good to be true. It's a trap. You're doomed. Jason stopped the barrage of negative thoughts with a force of will.

"How did you do that? I mean, easy enough to figure out my name I suppose, but, I've been gone for a while."

"No kidding! What's it like to work for Ambassador Shiny? Your life must be so exciting. I do nothing but flit here and there among the Core Worlds."

"How do you... you're very connected."

"I am." She held out her hand. "Stracey Stalos."

Jason accepted her hand but forgot to shake it.

"You work for Guriti Nervous Integration, don't you?" he asked.

"I used to. Wow, did you look me up? Are you going to answer my question?" She smiled playfully at him, as if she knew he was feeling her out. She patiently retrieved her hand.

"Sorry, I... I'm trying to figure out what's common knowledge these days. Earth has changed so much!"

"Not really. A little bit better than before. Mostly, though, everyone gets what they want here. It's a great time to be alive. With more to come! Shiny has promised us immortality soon."

"Immortality? Tall order."

"He can do it. I believe him."

I wonder if that's achieved through Trilisk copies or some other means.

"Well, I'm not up to anything exciting," Jason said. "I'm cutting our ties with Parker Interstellar Travels."

"Which 'our' are you using there?"

"The real PIT team. We work for Shiny as you say... although we don't always love him as much as everyone else does. How is it that you like him? Immortality aside."

Stracey laughed. "Aside from immortality! Well, he gives us what we want. He doesn't take the lion's share for himself."

"Oh he's got the lion's share," Jason said. "But I suppose what's left over now is still a lot more than what was left over before. He's got more than the Earth government ever had."

Stracey shook her head. "It's so weird that you're harshing on him. You're the ones who should like him. The PIT team fought the Space Force to bring him here for our own good. His personal... what are you exactly?"

"Explorers," Jason said carefully.

Stracey looked at Jason intensely in a way that made him feel wonderful and uncomfortable at the same time.

"What does Core World Security want with you?" she asked.

"Hrm, what?" Jason stuttered.

"I just received a request stamped from CWS asking me to leave you. They want to speak with you alone."

"I'm here to meet with them, I just didn't think they'd get back to me so quickly."

"You said you weren't up to anything," she told him over a link connection. "I can't blame you though... CWS... a man with secrets." Her voice sounded encouragingly positive.

"Please don't be put off by CWS. I'd like to have dinner with you," he replied in private. Both of them glanced around, wondering if they were being observed by security agents.

"Oh, if anything it makes you even more interesting. I'll meet you."

"Hopefully I'll be free later tonight."

"Then I'll wait for your message."

Stracey walked away with a sly smile on her face that took his breath away. He stood for a second, processing his amazement. All too quickly, his mind turned to the negatives.

I was thinking of her earlier... now she shows up. She said she was looking for me. Is that a case of mutual infatuation, or... has Shiny gotten so good at using the AI that it actually makes things like this happen... do people's wishes come true here?

Jason's face clouded. He stepped off the causeway to an observation niche over the streets below.

Is that why everyone is happy now? Or is this just coincidence? Maybe she was just snooping for information.

"Cthulhu's slimy hand! I have to tell Telisa."

"Tell her what?" a woman said, stepping up next to Jason. She wore a red dress and had bright pink, wavy hair.

"A theory about Shiny," Jason said, telling the truth without revealing much.

"I'm Agent Starlathi. Please follow me a short way so we can speak privately?"

Jason nodded. They continued down the conveyor and took the next walk-off exit. Jason spotted a camera ball floating by the entrance.

"Press?" he asked the agent via link.

"No, that's ours," she replied. They walked past the ball toward large glass doors. Her red dress turned black as they walked inside, proving it to be a reusable dress rather than a Core World disposable. Jason supposed CWS might need to wear things more durable in case they encountered trouble.

Trouble on Earth is a lot different than trouble on the frontier.

They walked through a lobby that Jason thought must contain extra security, though he could not see any clues of it. Then they continued through a side hallway and entered a meeting room. Jason threw off a sense of claustrophobia that had to derive from his thoughts about CWS and the security of the building.

A man stood up from across the table. He nodded. "Jason. I'm Agent Trebok."

"Hello," Jason said. He sighed and took a seat. His link showed many convenience services such as food and drink. He asked for an ice water.

"We were surprised to receive your request to meet," Starlathi said. She sat down an equal distance from Jason and Agent Trebok.

"I want to ask you about Shiny," Jason said. "If you have questions of your own, I'll do my best to trade information with you."

A small robot delivered Jason's water. He looked at it and wondered if the flimsy machine could paralyze him if the agents ordered it to do so. He decided it probably could not, but supposed that a hidden stunner might be trained on him from the ceiling or the table.

Starlathi took the lead. "What do you want to know about Shiny?"

"Why does everyone love him?"

Starlathi looked bemused.

"That's the question? Well, assuming you're serious... he replaced an alien regime that controlled Earth. They imprisoned many citizens and deprived others of resources. Ambassador Shiny freed everyone and has provided huge amounts of new resources for free. He enforces almost no laws beyond personal security and protection of property. In a nutshell, everyone is better off now than before in almost every way."

"But he took over by force. Now he is loved. Isn't that suspicious?"

"No. When he took over by force I felt that was a bad sign, but my fears proved unfounded."

Hrm. Maybe. I should try to be a bit more abrasive and see if I get anywhere.

"Does CWS have mind control weapons?"

"How is that relevant?"

"Shiny has Trilisk technology. I think he's used that to make everyone like him."

"Then I have to ask: why didn't everyone love the UN before he arrived? The Trilisks were running the show here. If they had that technology, wouldn't they have been using it too?"

"The Trilisks here may have been greatly weakened by war. I know of at least one thing Shiny had that the Trilisks here may not have had access to: A powerful Trilisk artifact that came from somewhere else."

Starlathi digested that while Trebok finally spoke up.

"If he does, then you'd now love him too, yes? Surely he would use this mind control device on his own elite team?"

"Good point," Jason said. "How long did it take for everyone to warm to Shiny after the takeover?"

The two agents looked at each other. Jason did not get the feeling they were discussing whether or not to reveal something. He interpreted it as simple recollection and uncertainty at the odd line of questioning.

"It took a month at least. It wasn't immediate, if that's what you're thinking," Starlathi said.

Jason thought about stopping there. Dare he expose his latest theory to them?

"How has life been for you? Personally," Jason asked.

Starlathi frowned.

"It is relevant, I assure you," Jason said. "Have things been going your way? Agent Trebok. How about you? You happy? Been achieving goals? Catching some lucky breaks?"

"Things are well with me. Why?" Trebok said.

Jason looked at Starlathi.

"I'm doing well."

"Did you get something you wanted? Promotion? Vacation?"

The two exchanged looks.

"Are you saying that the... exuberance Earthers have been experiencing are the result of Ambassador Shiny's Trilisk technology?"

"Earthers have been exuberant?"

"Yes. As it turns out, the mood here on Earth is markedly improved. Very significantly," Starlathi said. "I'm not speaking anecdotally, either. The stats have been analyzed by AIs. Something changed. We attribute it to the revolution, the removal of the Trilisks, and the sudden abundance of resources."

"Is it more than resources? Have you been catching lucky breaks?"

"I have," Trebok offered. "I wanted the opportunity to study with an idol of mine, and it recently came to pass."

Jason turned to Starlathi. She did not say anything.

"Well, have things gone well with you too?" he prompted.

Starlathi looked down at the table.

"Yes, things have gone well for me, several things, since Ambassador Shiny took over," Starlathi said.

Jason nodded. He mused out loud.

"When you make progress, when things go your way, you just want more though, right? It's human nature."

Starlathi changed the subject.

"Are you offering to be an inside source on the PIT team?"

"Not secretly. Telisa knows I'm here. It's in our best interest to cooperate, though. We're all Terrans here. The universe has gotten a lot bigger, so we should all work together to keep humanity safe."

"What alien threats are there?"

"Trilisks, of course. Also, the race that destroyed Shiny's homeworld. We just call them Destroyers."

"What is the PIT team doing now? What's your next objective?"

Why aren't they asking more about the Destroyers?

"We're investigating another race. Potential allies we call the Celarans. They were advanced creatures, capable of changing planetary ecosystems and climates for colonization. I don't know if they are ahead or behind where the Vovokans were, but I think if we can find any of them that are left, it could be key to securing our safety."

"We'd like to set up a method for you to make regular reports to CWS," Trebok said.

Jason nodded. "That sounds wise," he said, though he felt distracted. All he could think about was his dinner with Stracey Stalos.

***

"I'm glad you agreed to meet me," Jason said as he walked up to Stracey's table in a beautiful restaurant. They had a room to themselves, the ultimate arrangement for incarnate dining in the city. A breathtaking unaugmented view of the night skyline dominated one wall through real windows.

"My pleasure."

"Please forgive me if I get right to it then."

"Please do. I'm intrigued," she said. "You said the subject was Ambassador Shiny."

"Yes. Why is he so popular?"

Her eyebrows rose. Jason was struck by her beauty again. The look just made her more gorgeous.

"He's popular because he's made everything better for us here. What kind of question is that, coming from a member of his famous PIT team?" She asked with a playful tone.

"Look at it from our perspective. We came here to save Earth and watched as Shiny took over. We left the system in shame, traitors to our race. Now we're heroes? How did that happen?"

"The people of Earth didn't realize the Trilisks had taken over. The masses are always buried in their entertainments. Once we learned that Ambassador Shiny really is a liberator, not an alien bent on domination, we came to see you as heroes. I'm sorry no one welcomed you that way in the beginning."

Jason had to concentrate to keep from just staring at Stracey instead of listening to her answers, as important as they were.

"Shiny could have rid you of the Trilisks without taking over."

"No. There would have been chaos. Maybe even a new war with the UED. The Ambassador took over by force at first, sure, because he had to. Now, we know he only wants what's best for us."

"Shiny wants what's best for Shiny," he said.

Stracey listened carefully, but she looked confused. *Does she wonder if this is some kind of test?*

"I'm not sure the evidence supports that," she said carefully.

"I have the inside view. Shiny thinks it's worth keeping us happy for now, but he might change his mind later."

"Are you trying to convince me? Or did you just want to understand why Earthers love Ambassador Shiny?"

Jason shook his head. "Mostly I wanted to know why you feel the way you do. But I guess part of me can't help but want to warn you about him."

"Well, GNI wants to work with him. With the PIT team."

Jason's heart dropped.

Of course. She doesn't like me. She's just another person who wants to be on the PIT team and she sees me as a way to do that.

"The PIT team isn't hiring," he said coldly.

Stracey laughed. "Oh, Cthulhu knows I couldn't be on the PIT team like you," she said. "Do I look like some kind of explorer? This is almost the only reusable piece of clothing I own. I hang out in paper suits and attend meetings half the day. I just want to help in any way I can."

Jason relaxed a notch. Maybe she had some hidden agenda or maybe she did not. The fact she was highly placed in a large corporation spoke for the former, though.

"I appreciate the offer. I'll pass it on to Telisa, but Shiny pretty much gets us whatever we need. I'm not sure what a company like GNI could—"

Jason stopped. He had been thinking about GNI giving them new links or enhancing some of their wetware. A new thought struck him dumb.

Nervous system experts. And we do have a huge nervous system problem—how to keep Telisa from being remotely controlled by Trilisks.

"Something important?" Stracey asked. She assumed he had been interrupted by an off-retina input.

"I'll speak with Telisa Relachik about the possibility," Jason finished. "We might be able to use your expertise."

"I can ask for nothing more," she said. "Except, perhaps, a nightcap?"

"Uhm, yes," he said slowly. He realized he sounded less than enthusiastic, so continued, "Sure. That would be nice."

Chapter 19

Telisa changed her position on the lounge for the fourteenth time. Jason's short message had sent her into new lines of thought: Did Shiny actually use the Trilisk AI to cause things to happen that made billions of Terrans happier? On a citizen-by-citizen basis? As incredible as it sounded, Telisa knew better than to underestimate the technology of the Trilisks. Those beings had ascended to incredible power long before the rise of Terra.

I need someone who could cut through the hype and really let me know the situation on Earth.

Jason's assessment of the opinions from two CWS agents did not help much. It had been worth a shot, but the agents were not someone at the top, privy to secrets, and they did not seem like people who had asked the same question in depth.

Why does Earth love Shiny so much?

Her father had given her information on his Space Force friend Nick Vrolyk. She decided to use it. The man was a career officer who must have achieved a high rank by now.

Telisa asked for a link channel to Vrolyk. The connection went through with both audio and video feeds. The metadata told her Vrolyk was now an admiral in the Space Force. Telisa felt her hopes for an inside secret rise. The man she saw looked older, perhaps Cilreth's age. His head was angular, bordered by patches of light brown hair. She searched his face for hatred or disdain, but he seemed simply curious.

"Telisa! I never thought to hear from you. Tell me Leonard found his way to you before the end."

"He did. We reconciled."

Remembering his death brought back a stab of pain, but it had faded with time.

"That's good. I should have known he would succeed. He was determined. A great man," Vrolyk said. The video feed showed Vrolyk look aside, salute, and dismiss someone off the feed. Then he continued.

"And, you're an amazing woman by all accounts. I don't mean to sound cliche, but I have no doubt he was proud of your achievements. What can I do for you, Telisa?"

"I'd like to meet with you incarnate."

Admiral Vrolyk pursed his lips and nodded. "Very well, I'm at your disposal."

"Really? You aren't a busy man?"

"Well, you're a Relachik. But there's more to it than that. Let's just say you're a personality that's important to the Space Force."

"You want to arrest me?"

"Honestly, I don't know what we'd do with you, but in any case, we can't touch you as long as Ambassador Shiny controls Earth. You're on a 'no-touch' list."

"What do you know about Admiral Sager?"

"He's as good as they come."

"Do you see eye to eye with him?"

"About what?"

"Alien overlords."

Nick stared hard at Telisa, then nodded. "Yes."

"Then I'd like to meet with you as soon as possible, and if Sager wants in, he's welcome there. This connection doesn't show where you are."

"I'm at Space Force Command. I can send a high speed transport for you, wherever you are."

"Then send one. I'll be ready."

The Admiral nodded and dropped the connection. Vrolyk quickly put a meeting on her schedule and she approved it immediately.

***

"Cilreth. How's it going?" Telisa asked. She stretched in the center of her hotel room and flexed her enhanced muscles.

"Your timing is perfect. I need your help."

"Yes?"

"I found our newbie," Cilreth reported. "He's inside a fortress with security. We have to get in there."

"Doesn't sound like a newbie to me. We can't just ask nicely?"

"I'd rather make an impression."

Telisa laughed. "It could backfire. We could make an enemy."

"With enemies like Shiny, who needs friends?"

"I'm not sure I even understand what you just said. But sure, I'll help you get in there. After I meet a Space Force admiral."

"Admiral? Wow, okay. Well tell me when your busy schedule opens up, Lady Relachik."

Telisa ignored the barb. "How about first thing tomorrow?"

"Perfect."

"Oh wait. One more thing. I gave my stealth device to Imanol. Long story. So we'll have to get in there the old fashioned way."

"Well actually, I was thinking Trilisk Special Forces style."

"Oh! Okay, that works too. See you tomorrow."

***

A few hours later, Telisa took a sleek new shuttle to Space Force Command. The ride was quick and comfortable, with many automated services available for food, drink, or entertainment. Telisa allowed herself to relax until she arrived. When the shuttle landed, she exited the shuttle onto a large, glossy concourse. A female attache met her on the concourse.

"Welcome to Space Force Command. Telisa Relachik?" the person asked politely. She looked intensely interested in Telisa.

"Yes. I'm here to see Admiral Vrolyk."

"This way, please!" the woman replied enthusiastically. They had barely taken three steps in the indicated direction when she stepped beside Telisa and started to talk.

"It's fantastic to have you here. Do you have an official rank in the Space Force, Miss Relachik?"

"I don't believe so," Telisa said.

"Well, it doesn't matter does it? Admiral Vrolyk doesn't have many meetings with civilians. But you're the leader of the first of Shiny's special teams! It must be an exciting lifestyle."

"It can be," Telisa said haltingly. "How many teams does Shiny have these days? I've been out of system for a while."

"No one knows. But everyone speaks of at least four or five. It's so hard to know for sure, some of them must be fake. Shiny doesn't verify things. We can observe the behavior of his security drones and see who they follow. One time we thought someone was one of his people but it was actually an insane person who planned to hurt people. The drones were just waiting to intervene."

They had arrived at the entrance to an elevator. They stepped in next to an officer. The attache stopped talking. The officer seemed to recognize Telisa with a start. He straightened up, took a step back, and gave her more space.

"Your Veer suit has seen some action!" the attache said from slightly behind Telisa's left shoulder.

"Yes. I engaged... we engaged an alien war machine. Did something hit me back there? My suit's diagnostic is showing full integrity."

The attache gasped.

Maybe I should have been more vague.

The officer said, "Cosmetic damage only, miss. If Momma Veer says the suit is still good, I'd bank my life on it."

Telisa could not resist an embellishment.

"As long as it hasn't been hacked by CWS again."

The officer covered a laugh with a fake cough. The attache beamed.

The elevator opened.

"We're here, Miss Relachik," the attache said. They walked out into an automated reception area. The attache led Telisa to an office. Inside, Admiral Vrolyk stood waiting. Since Telisa was not in the Space Force, she did not salute.

Admiral Vrolyk did salute. He stood frozen with his hand in place, so Telisa returned it.

"Good to meet you, ma'am" Vrolyk said. He stood at attention.

"That's not necessary, Admiral, I'm not in the Space Force."

The Admiral cleared his throat. "Thank you, ma'am, but I am required to salute my superiors in most circumstances."

"How's it I'm your superior?"

"Shiny delivered an extremely detailed set of protocols and guidelines when he... when he was installed as our ruler."

"Oh?"

"Those guidelines included some very high ranking individuals placed above the admiralty. Of which you are one."

Telisa absorbed that.

So, I'm some super-officer of the Space Force? Should I scoff that off? Have to think about it.

"At ease, then," Telisa said.

The admiral's shoulders dropped just a bit and he took a step back.

"I can see your father in you, if I may say so."

Vrolyk stood taller than Telisa expected. She looked up at his rough face.

"He told me you're a good man. I need someone I can trust. By the way, why didn't the attache mention my rank and salute me?"

"It's not exactly common knowledge. We released a lot of his demands to the public, but not everything. If you wish, I'll inform all Space Force personnel of your position immediately."

"Shiny didn't see fit to release the details himself?"

"No ma'am. Admiral Sager is almost here," he said. Telisa heard a sound behind her as he spoke. She turned a bit too fast, startling Sager, who had just entered. He saluted her.

"At ease," Telisa repeated.

"Apologies, ma'am," Sager said. "I meant no disrespect."

"Admiral Sager. Glad to see you made it."

"Yes, ma'am." He seemed hesitant.

"Feel free to ask questions here," she said.

"What have you been up to? No one's been able to find you," Sager said. They took seats at the table.

"I left the system in shame."

"So you really were taken by surprise?"

"Shiny's takeover shocked me. I don't know why. I suppose I'm guilty of the cardinal sin of anthropomorphization."

Which hurts, because I'm supposed to study alien civilizations.

"So what are you up to now?"

"I want to know how Shiny has managed to solidify his hold over Earth's population. I want to know who's for him and who's really against him."

"That's odd coming from one of his people," Vrolyk said.

"I'm not convinced he earned himself a place as our supreme overlord, whether he saved us from the Trilisks or not."

"And your own rank?"

"I don't intend to use it, for the most part. Except perhaps where it might speed up my own modest projects."

They nodded.

"Do you accept him as your leader? Does the rest of the admiralty? The men and women you command?"

"At first the entire organization railed against the takeover," Vrolyk said. "It wasn't a matter of if we would rebel, it was when and how. We have extensive plans in that direction. But our resolve to follow through faded away. We don't want to sacrifice our men and women trying to throw off an alien that has proven so valuable to us."

He's being pretty honest. If I had plans like that, I doubt I'd mention it to me. Is that because he knew my father, or something else?

"So he allows the Space Force free rein?" she asked.

"Yes, as long as we don't interfere with him or his facilities. He keeps law and order on Earth."

"What about the other Core Worlds?"

"They're scared. And they want us to strike against him," Vrolyk said.

"Okay, then let's forget about who's for him and who's against him. How the hell did he become so popular? Is it mind control?"

"It's a possibility," Vrolyk said without hesitation. "The problem is, if we're being externally convinced he's a good dictator, how can we act against that? Why would we? I personally feel he's been one of the best things that's happened to us in a long time. Ever since the destruction of the *Seeker*, I've feared for the fate of every Terran."

"What are you afraid of?" Telisa asked.

"The Destroyers and other aliens out there," Sager said.

"You know about them?" Telisa said. Her voice gave away her surprise more strongly than she would have liked.

"Shiny said these things devastated the Vovokan homeworld."

"I've been there," Telisa said. "Or at least, someplace where Vovokans lived that had been hit hard, and the Destroyers were there."

"The Ambassador has given us changes for the weapons of our starships. He says the alterations will give us some minor ability to damage these aliens."

"He doesn't have enough of his own starships?" Telisa asked. "Why doesn't he make more?"

"We think he is," Sager said. "And we've asked ourselves the same questions. Our scientists and engineers admit the suggestions are good, at least, they increase our destructive capacity."

"What else did he tell you about the Destroyers?" Telisa asked.

Sager hesitated.

"I have information of my own to offer you," Telisa said. "About a race we call the Celarans. They seem peaceful, but not so peaceful they don't defend themselves. I've been trying to make contact with them."

Telisa sent Sager and Vrolyk a pointer. They accessed an information module about the Celarans that she had prepared.

"Do you know of them?" she asked.

"Your teammate Caden Lonrack mentioned them in passing. He did not say much. Ambassador Shiny has only told us of the Destroyers, the Trilisks, and more vaguely, of an ancient enemy to the Trilisks."

"What do you know about the Destroyers?" Telisa asked.

This time Sager replied, though in a distracted manner, as he checked Telisa's information off-retina.

"Originally an aquatic race," Vrolyk said. "They manipulated their environment electrically and chemically as much as in courser physical ways in their rise from primitive times. Very different from us, as you might expect, rising to power without the use of fire. We were surprised at the Ambassador's honesty here, or presumed honesty, in that he basically admitted the Destroyers were friendly at first, but thanks to the aggressive actions of a Vovokan faction, they're now extreme xenophobes. He says that's why we have to be afraid of them."

"Of course I wonder if we could make friends with them, if we met them in Terran ships without any Vovokans around," Telisa said.

"My thoughts exactly, but Ambassador Shiny assured us that the Destroyers are now extremely paranoid about all aliens, not just Vovokans."

"Then my mission is more important than ever before. We need to find the Celarans, if they still exist. We need to become allies with them."

"I see a solution to at least two of our problems," Sager said. "Allow us to send an ambassador with you. We can take him aboard the *Midway*. I'll take command and personally guarantee our behavior. We'll lend protection to your mission, help these Celarans, or fight the Destroyers. And I'll be far from Earth, where we can see if my attitude towards Shiny's takeover changes."

Telisa digested the idea in silence.

"The *Midway*? A large space force ship?"

"A new flagship."

"Midway between what and what?" Telisa asked.

Sager smiled. "Named after an ancient battle."

Telisa nodded.

Chapter 20

Telisa and Cilreth stood on a lone platform amid a series of mountains in Lesser Brazil, on the west coast of South America. Telisa felt the sun warm on her face, though the clean air blew cold and crisp across the platform. A covered passenger area at the edge of the gray platform was directly behind them. Beyond that niche, visible through a thick transparent plate, a cliff dropped precipitously. The open air below was broken only by the huge carbon struts that supported the structure and the cable car line that had brought them up.

An elegant shuttle sat on a landing pad before them. It was too small for a gravity spinner, so it used four large encased fans for lift. Its gray and turquoise surface appeared smooth and clean with few seams. Its shape was less boxy than most transports, more streamlined. Telisa guessed it might only carry ten or twelve passengers. She could not see anyone else in or around the shuttle. Forty attendant spheres patrolled the area above and below the platform.

Telisa felt the heft of her laser rifle across her back. She had decided to bring a little extra power just in case. She had traded in her smart pistol for a pair of stun pistols, since she doubted she wanted to kill anyone. Her breaker claw was hidden away in an inside pocket of her Veer suit along with a tanto knife.

"We're way over-armed for Earth, mentally and physically. I think this is what soldiers feel like when they come back from war," Cilreth said.

"I'll make sure to ask Magnus someday," Telisa said. Cilreth nodded and did not continue the line of conversation.

She probably won't touch that. I'm too sensitive about him and no one will mention him to me.

Cilreth shared a video feed of the exterior of Marcant's sanctuary from a distant attendant. The feed showed a sprawling two-story concrete structure with VTOL landing zones marked across its flat top. A ghostly blueprint flipped on, overlaying the feed. It showed a deep complex with many layers beneath. It reminded Telisa of a private factory owned by a megacorporation.

"Cilreth. Why is our new recruit in a fortress?" asked Telisa.

"He's got a lot of friends. And he's well known in certain circles."

"Well known as in..."

"As in a lot of people might want to get their hands on him. Like us. Except for different reasons."

"A lot of friends and a lot of enemies. Fair enough. So why are we here instead of over there?" Telisa asked.

"This is the only shuttle route in and out," Cilreth said. "The other approaches are protected by air defenses. Damping fields, interceptor clamps, all kinds of things."

"I'm sure they have other escape routes," Telisa said. "Let's get some help locking them down."

"How?"

"I have very high authority with Shiny's security forces," Telisa said offered playfully.

"You're becoming corrupt," Cilreth said. "Don't do it."

"Are we getting him or not?"

"We will. Without direct help from Shiny. Do you want Marcant with us, or do you simply expect him to capitulate to Shiny?"

"He's worth it right?" Telisa asked.

"Yes, if we can convince him. I think if we do it without Shiny's overt help, he's more likely to join us."

Telisa told ten attendants to encircle the fortress at high altitude. Cilreth watched them fly off.

"Okay, we'll know if someone escapes by air and I'll just track them," Telisa said. "No Vovokan battle spheres. Better?"

"Yes."

"So I assume we're taking control of this shuttle?" she asked.

"We could. But that's plan B," Cilreth said.

"Okay. What's plan A?"

"Another shuttle is coming in," Cilreth said. "We'll catch a ride on it because it's expected. We might be able to get over to the main facility before they know something's wrong."

"It's unmanned?"

"They have security guards on board," Cilreth told her.

Telisa sighed. "Of course," she said. Though her voice sounded tired, she actually welcomed some action. She had not had a chance to train, virtually or incarnate, for a few days.

"Five minutes," Cilreth said.

Telisa nodded. She paced the landing platform and waited.

When the shuttle approached, Telisa and Cilreth backed up to wait in the passenger area. The shuttle looked just like the first. It landed on the other side of the open platform. Telisa thought perhaps four such shuttles could land here, but the way the shuttles had positioned themselves in the center of each side, they blocked any other possible landings.

Telisa and Cilreth approached the new shuttle. Cilreth talked to the shuttle through her link. At first nothing happened. Then a short, stocky man walked out of the shuttle and headed toward them. He spoke aloud in another language but Telisa's link fed her the speech so she could understand it.

"I'm sorry, but there must be a mix-up," he said.

"No mix-up, we're last minute passengers," Telisa said.

The man just shook his head. "I can't take you."

"Your friend knows me," Cilreth said. The man gave her a blank stare. Cilreth pointed at the shuttle.

"Your friend," she repeated. The man stood still, but he must have called to someone on his link. Another man walked around the side of the shuttle and approached them. He was also short, with a big mustache sprawling under his nose. Two attendants dropped from the sky and hovered over the men.

"I don't know you," said the other man.

"I've isolated their links," Cilreth said. "As far as this shuttle is concerned, we're them now."

Telisa casually drew her stunners, one in each hand, and dropped the men in one second. The attendants verified they were still breathing.

"And the video feeds?"

"I'll put something together," Cilreth said. "For now, I'll just show it empty. We can go on inside."

They boarded the shuttle. Telisa saw two passengers in the back, busy off-retina. She shrugged and sat in the control compartment with Cilreth.

"Are they dangerous?" Cilreth asked.

"You worry about the shuttle and get us over there," Telisa said. She listened to the breathing of the man and woman in the section behind them. Her enhanced senses even allowed her to smell each of them. She detected nothing threatening.

"With them back there, there's less chance the shuttle will be diverted or brought down," she sent to Cilreth silently. "Are they really going to let their shuttle fly us over?"

Cilreth's blank expression hinted at off-retina activity. Telisa assumed she managed their route off-retina.

"Well, it's our shuttle now," Cilreth said. "Er, uhm... *now*," she corrected, flustered.

"What was that?" Telisa asked.

"Tricky dynamic security," Cilreth said. "I took over all the processors and they almost all flipped back. Without the Vovokan support I don't think I could have done it at all."

"How can they flip back if you already had them all?"

"They're still flipping, but I'm on top of it now. There's a hidden set of nodes here that secure the public ones. I'm rooting them out. Small chance they've been alerted that something's up. I control the main communications, but if there are hidden nodes they might have a backup comm line."

"What? Hurry it up, then," Telisa urged.

"Hrmph. No appreciation. Let's go."

The shuttle lifted off the pad and flew off toward a break in the nearby mountains. Telisa continued to listen in on the passengers as the small craft hurled along.

"Countermeasures are being deployed. They know," Cilreth said.

"How could they know? The hidden comm line?" Telisa asked.

"Maybe. We're also on some video and microphone feeds. I made us look like those guys in the feeds, but I couldn't get every detail perfect. Those feeds were analyzed and something or someone could have come to the conclusion that we aren't who we say we are," Cilreth sent back. "The way everything was put together, there's probably an AI involved."

Makes sense that someone like Marcant has an AI on security detail.

"Can we get through?"

"We will," Cilreth said.

Telisa saw objects approaching from far ahead. Her acute sight picked up details from the high resolution feeds. The devices looked like flying C-shaped metal pincers with heavy magnetic pads along the inside.

"Interceptor clamps," Telisa said.

"Yes. On it."

As Cilreth spoke, a small squadron of attendants flew in and disabled them. The clamps fell from the sky, dead.

The mountain complex grew as they zeroed in on the landing areas. Telisa caught sight of a handful of people walking or working around the buildings, but none of them seemed alarmed. Within another two minutes, Cilreth had set them down atop the fortress.

The passengers in the back of the shuttle remained unaware of the situation. Telisa watched them walk out. She had no reason to view them as a threat. Once the passengers were clear, Telisa and Cilreth walked outside. The passengers were going through a checkpoint at the side of the landing area.

The checkpoint had two large ovals for people and cargo to pass through, likely equipped with deep scanning capability. To either side of the loops sat an armored desk. Telisa saw a man or an android standing behind the desk on the right.

"Well they're not shooting at us," Telisa said.

"Yet," Cilreth qualified. "They may have expected the clamps to work. I imagine more security is on its way."

Telisa remained calm and strode up to the entrance. The guard looked first surprised, then almost alarmed as he either recognized Telisa or received a warning in his link.

Not an android.

"We're here to see Marcant," Telisa said matter-of-factly.

The man looked straight at Telisa with a frown on his face.

"No such person here. A squad will escort you back out to the landing platform, miss."

"You're not even going to contact Marcant and ask?"

The man simply drew his weapon. Cilreth bristled. Telisa saw the weapon was a stunner. Two other men became visible from behind the armored desks, one on each side. They looked determined and ready for action, though they did not display weapons over the high desks.

"It's not worth risking any deaths just to see Marcant," Cilreth sent her.

"Not a risk taker?" Telisa teased. "Nonlethal weapons here, the risk of collateral damage is still low."

Telisa moved in a blur. She launched herself over the desk on the right, rolling in the air along her arc. All three of the men had been disarmed in two seconds. A black spot flowered on the ground where Telisa had started. The laser, though probably capable of aiming faster, had not been configured for superhuman speed. Telisa leaped four meters straight upwards and smashed the laser emitter dome with her fist. The dome took her hit squarely. It deformed a bit but remained intact. She dropped back to her feet.

"Okay, I'm not *that* strong," she told Cilreth through their link connection.

Telisa rolled forward and sheltered under the armored desk. She accessed her breaker claw. It actuated on the laser just as the desktop above her started to change color from the intense heat. There was no explosion. Telisa figured that meant the emplacement's storage ring had already been mostly emptied by the laser.

Telisa stood and waved Cilreth forward.

"I could have been killed by the laser," Cilreth said, but her voice did not sound truly concerned.

"It would never have engaged a non-combatant."

"We're far from any city or any of Shiny's forces. We don't know if things are going to be nice and civil out here."

Telisa wondered if Cilreth had a point. Earth's own government had collapsed. Would that mean that the veneer of civilization had cracked? Telisa had experienced entertainment VRs about what might happen if large groups of people were put into danger. The theory was, everyone would quickly become capable of monstrous acts in order to survive. Shiny had kept the peace in most places with the help of Earth's own infrastructure, but as Cilreth said, they were off the beaten path.

Telisa decided to shrug it off.

"Then stay sharp and stay close. It's a chance for a bit of incarnate training."

"We're outed, so I'll start cracking this place electronically," Cilreth said. "Here's a more trustworthy map than we had before. It's what these guys use, so more likely to be accurate than what the public records had."

Telisa accessed the map. Cilreth had selected a route deeper into the complex, so Telisa overlayed it onto her retinal input and ran ahead.

"You're as fast as the shuttle we came in on," Cilreth said, falling behind.

"Hurry up. It'll be good for you," Telisa replied in good humor.

Telisa came to a T-shaped intersection at the end of the entrance terminal. She took a superhumanly quick peek.

"Security machines," she warned Cilreth. Then she darted past the corner, charging a machine in the right corridor. The machine acquired her in a split second and opened fire. A self-guiding soft projectile, meant to stun, arced toward her with two grenades following it.

Telisa leaped through the air at the security machine. An attendant, itself struggling to keep up, intercepted the soft round. Telisa batted aside the two grenades mid-flight with her bare hands, then landed next to the robot. She squatted to the floor, grasped its legs, and stood again, taking the heavy legs with her. The machine flipped over onto its back and landed with a crash.

Cilreth turned the corner just in time to witness Telisa disable the machine by pulling off its sensor-encrusted head with her bare hands. The two grenades had flowered into large glue clusters that looked like ugly beige anemones.

"Now what?" Telisa said.

"I've wreaked havoc with these systems," Cilreth said, stepping carefully around the glue clusters. "They may be able to track us anyway. With an AI, it's hard to gauge what it can do."

They ran past the dead machine on a wide, glossy gray floor with veins like marble. They passed a series of personal studios on their right, many equipped with partial VR equipment. One of them was alive with wall displays broadcast through their links. Telisa did not stay long enough to see what was being shown.

"Keep a lookout. There was probably someone in there," Telisa said.

As she spoke, she caught sight of movement. Some kind of robot moved through an intersection ahead of her. Telisa used her breaker claw just in case. The small robot stopped dead in the middle of the floor.

"Righteous kill," Cilreth said. "I think that was a repair machine."

"Better safe than sorry. Stay sharp." Telisa ran ahead to the intersection, leaving Cilreth behind again. She could hear her companion panting behind her as they ran. To Telisa, their pace was sluggish. She felt like moving faster, working harder.

It will suck if I have to go back to being my old self. But I would do it for him.

Telisa sent one attendant down each of the three corridors, leaving only one behind for herself. Two of them did not find anything of interest. There were a few scientists or engineers about in the building, and a handful of harmless robots. The third attendant fed her a view of a larger machine. It patrolled a set of long, wide corridors with smooth, shiny floors.

If there's more security, there must be something to keep secure.

"Another security machine," Telisa warned. She headed for the guarded corridors and sent Cilreth an indication of her intended path. She recalled the other two attendants to join her.

The machine was a small tank. Its bottom edges had an armored apron. It moved smoothly. Telisa figured it must have treads underneath, or perhaps it was a hovercraft, but it was too swift and too smooth to be on legs.

Telisa burst around a corner, aimed her laser rifle, and fired at the machine, aiming for a bulge she assumed was a sensor bubble. It took the hit.

Deception. Where are the sensors? I should aim for the center armor plate. Or the treads.

Telisa did not have time to stand idle any longer. Soon Cilreth would be in the field of fire.

"Old fashioned way, I guess," she said. Telisa shot forward. Then she lost her footing in an instant. Something was wrong. Telisa slid by the machine on the shiny floor, spinning out of control.

"By the Five!" Telisa exclaimed through the link.

The machine spun on a dime and headed after her. Telisa heard a loud whine and felt a slight wind. She rebounded off a wall and went flying the other direction.

"That machine uses a turbine for thrust," Cilreth sent back. Telisa flopped around on the far side of the hall. Her limbs slipped over the surface, unable to gain any purchase.

"What's wrong?"

"Floor... no friction!" Telisa said. Telisa lined her feet against the wall and pushed. She burst away from the wall, sliding on her back. She went by the robot again. The machine shot at her twice, but each time an attendant intercepted the projectile. Telisa managed to catch the edge of the machine and grab onto it. She pulled herself up with raw strength.

Okay even Trilisk Special Forces is feeling this one.

The machine whipped her about. For a moment she worried if it was going to smash her against a wall.

I can't use the breaker claw. This thing might have a big storage ring. I would just blow myself up.

Telisa forgot about a possible impact and focused on the machine. She wrapped one powerful hand around the projectile barrel in front of her and bent it. The laser rifle flopped about on her back. In fact, the strap was almost choking her as the machine continued a tight circle.

"Telisa! There's another one coming!"

Telisa hung on with one incredibly strong arm and lugged the rifle around with her other. She had an attendant feed the rifle a target sig and told it to fire on opportunity. At first nothing happened. The world swung around crazily. Eventually, the other machine came into the rifle's arc of fire. The rifle output a tenth of its energy in one invisible blast.

"It was no good," Cilreth said. Telisa's partner showed up on the tactical just around the corner. Telisa supposed that Cilreth must be monitoring the battle via the attendant feeds.

Telisa's Veer suit sent an alert. It was heating up rapidly under incoming laser energy. Telisa yelled in frustration and released her hold on the machine. She slid off to one side along the ultra slick floor. Then she used the breaker claw. She heard a loud crack and saw smoke, but she could not tell if the machine had sent out any shrapnel. Her Veer suit told her the laser had stopped, but it was registering a rupture in the torso. Telisa only felt a little bruised so she ignored it.

"I think the smoke is covering me," Telisa said.

"No, I got the attendants to push the other one off target," Cilreth said. "It has no real traction either, only the air thrust."

Telisa spotted the machine Cilreth spoke of. Three attendants pushed it in random loops. Telisa hit a wall hard. She exhaled, but the Veer suit had spread the impact anyway, so there was no real pain. Before she could rebound away, she pushed with her legs, frog-style, and shot forward toward the other tank, in the air.

Almost fun, once you know the game.

She told the rifle to hit it again with three charges worth while she was in the air. The second machine started to smoke. The sound of its turbine ceased. Though parts of it might still be functioning, it could not use its weapon or move under its own power. This time Telisa landed on her feet and slid across to another wall, pushed off, and reached a normal floor on the far side.

The attendants pushed the broken machines away and around a corner.

"Well, it may not be destroyed, but I think it's disabled," Telisa reported. "Thanks for keeping it from frying me, by the way."

"I'm not looking forward to trying to get over there."

"Just push off slowly on your butt and you'll make it... eventually," Telisa encouraged.

Cilreth got down on all fours and felt the floor where the surface change appearance. Her hand slipped across the floor so easily she almost fell forward comically just probing it. While Cilreth struggled to pass the frictionless zone, Telisa distracted her with chat.

"It's a clever system," Telisa said. "Anyone like us who muscles our way in here wouldn't be prepared for a zero-friction floor and a collection of turbine-powered guardians."

"What about flying attackers?"

"Must be rare. Flying through these corridors? I'm not sure. Maybe there's a trap somewhere for that, too."

Cilreth rebounded off one wall and then another, finally headed through the last corridor toward Telisa.

"You're bleeding!" Cilreth said out loud as she slid in. Telisa checked herself and saw dried blood on her left side where her suit had registered the hole. The suit had stopped the flow.

"I guess you're right. Something got through my attendants. It must have been pretty easy to plot my course while I was sliding around on the floor," Telisa said. "The suit is helping. Though I think it's confused by my physiology. I'm getting normal Terran doses of everything. I feel kind of weird."

"You have a bullet wound in your side! Of course you feel weird."

"Just be glad it was targeted to wound," Telisa said over the link, going silent again. "If they wanted me dead, I might be."

"I think you're underestimating the attendants."

Cilreth regained her feet carefully on the far side.

"I'll never trust the ground again," Cilreth said.

"I know what you mean."

They walked out into an atrium that connected several hallways on more than one level.

"Look. There are floors above us," Cilreth said. "Those floors are not on the schematic we snatched when we came in."

"How is that? I thought we came to a deeper level that went farther in this direction, but the building above did not."

"Well, there isn't any rule that says an underground building has to be shaped like a box. Especially inside a mountain. Those floors must be separated from the ones we came in on. The complex goes down from the shuttle entrance, then expands into the mountain, and his part forms a niche in the rock above us."

"So we go back up," Telisa said. "If it's not on the map used by the entrance guards, it must be interesting."

"They probably have an alternate escape route as you mentioned."

"Send some of the attendants in. If they can find shuttles, the attendants could disable them somehow."

"Well, we have the ones watching outside," Cilreth said.

"Yes, but this is getting a little personal," Telisa said, feeling her wound. "Let's get this guy's attention and move on."

Cilreth raised an eyebrow but she nodded.

"Lead the way."

"We'll go up there," Telisa said, pointing.

"Should I fire up a smart rope?"

Telisa leaped. Cilreth watched in awe as her friend soared upwards as if catapulted by an explosion. Telisa caught the railing of the next floor. She performed an overpowered chin-up, sending herself flying gracefully over the railing bar and landing squarely on her feet over the barrier.

Telisa paused there, looking for enemies. The balcony held comfortable perches that were each half chair, half sleeping web. Two exits led out to what she guessed were labs or meeting areas. She flipped through the various video feeds of the attendants flitting about and listened with her superhuman hearing.

"You make it?" Cilreth asked. Telisa sent down the smart rope in answer. It took a minute for Cilreth to take the smart rope up and join her. When she arrived, they looked upwards again. From the first balcony, the curve of the balcony above denied Telisa another direct jump. She would have to travel outwards, upwards, then back inwards in mid air to grab the next balcony rail.

"I don't think even Trilisk Special Forces can do this one," Cilreth said.

"Smart rope," Telisa said airily. She took the one Cilreth had ascended on and let it encircle an attendant. The attendant carried the end up to the next balcony, where the rope knotted itself onto a railing. The attendant flew on, looking for danger.

They moved up to the next balcony and assessed their position in the complex.

"I think Marcant is around here," Cilreth said out loud. "We're pretty deep into this place."

"You take the left side, I'll take the right."

"This is an awful lot of trouble for an interview," Cilreth said. Telisa grinned.

"We might have to glue him down just to get a conversation. Not a great first impression."

"I know what he wants. He'll accept the offer," Cilreth said. "Forget the left and right. An attendant has spotted a door near here that's heavily secured."

They walked ahead twenty meters to the metal door Cilreth had pointed out. It was a sliding metal door placed firmly in a thick frame of heavy ceramic armor.

"Too obvious? Is it a trap?" Telisa asked. She walked up to the door. Her sharp eyesight spotted tiny sensor buds on the wall around the door.

"I doubt it. I'm hacking our way in," Cilreth said.

Telisa did not dare touch the door. "We could circumvent it. I might be able to cut through the wall with my rifle, or my bare hands," Telisa said.

Cilreth had not yet answered when they received a link message.

"Please stop. The humiliation is quite agonizing," someone said. Her link connection identified the speaker as Marcant.

Telisa could not tell if the request was genuine or facetious.

"Okay. Let us in. We're only here to talk," Cilreth said.

The door slid open.

"You take it from here," Telisa said. "I'll make sure you have plenty of time with our elusive candidate."

Cilreth nodded. "Be careful."

"Always."

Chapter 21

Marcant watched video feeds off-retina in his room. He saw a strikingly beautiful woman step out of a shuttle and walk across a landing pad. It was not an entertainment VR, though the woman could have starred in one. It was a feed of what had been happening right outside his doors.

A laser mount tried to track her. She moved across the room faster than the emitter could follow and knocked out three men. As the emitter retargeted her, she leaped up and struck it. The video feed shook so hard that Marcant wondered if the emitter had been knocked out of alignment. Apparently the laser survived the attack, but the woman slid under the armored desk before it could hit her. Then the feed abruptly ceased.

Marcant skipped ahead to another video clip. He spotted her again, moving as a blur. He slowed the feed to watch her. The woman defeated two grenades in a half second, intercepting them and batting them away before the glue could flower over her.

What is she?

"Yes, what?" Adair asked. The AI was privy to his most private thoughts, integrated into his mind through his link. "And how can we stop her?"

"The other machines might stop her," Achaius said. Marcant had never heard such strong doubt in the voice of his aggressive AI companion.

"I believe that's an android copy of Telisa Relachik," said Adair. "That would explain—"

"All evidence indicates she is alive at a cellular level," Achaius interjected.

"It also shows she's not a mere Terran," Adair said.

"She's something made by technology superior to ours," Marcant said. "Something made by Ambassador Shiny. Whether she's still that woman Telisa Relachik, who knows?"

Marcant watched a feed of the woman skating through the zero-friction area and taking out his robots like she was playing a game of ice hockey against children.

She will make it here. Whatever she wants, she'll probably get.

He skipped to the next sighting. The two women were talking. Marcant listened in.

"This is an awful lot of trouble for an interview," the one called Cilreth said. Her companion smiled. Marcant found himself staring at Telisa again.

"We might have to glue him down just to get a conversation. Not a great first impression," she said.

"I know what he wants. He'll accept the offer," Cilreth said.

"They're crazy," Marcant breathed. "They just force their way in here casually. They're not the least bit fazed by our defenses."

"They don't want to hurt you," Achaius said. "It really is just an interview?"

"They might know we're watching," Adair said. "The conversation could have been for our benefit."

"Why? They can get in here and get me despite all precautions. And Shiny hasn't even lifted a... leg," Marcant said.

"They want your cooperation," Adair said. "Deception can be used instead of force. They might know you'll perform better that way."

"Shiny doesn't need me," Marcant said. "I can't even touch him. Why would they risk their lives to come here and talk to me?"

"Are their lives really at risk? We use mostly nonlethal measures here," Achaius said.

"*Mostly*. Besides, how do they know that?"

"I don't know, but they're playing along. They could have left a trail of death to our door," Adair said. "None of our personnel have died."

"We have to assume they'll make it up here and through the armored doors," Marcant said. "At least that one, the one we think is Telisa. I should prepare myself."

"We can set some nasty traps in here," Adair said. "Just give me the word. What do you want to do?"

"I'll cooperate."

Michael McCloskey

Chapter 22

Cilreth slipped into the room and told the door to lock behind her. She scanned the ceiling for lasers or other defenses. It looked safe, though she could not verify much in the poor light. She saw a bed hiding in a corner to her right, and what looked like the doorway to a closet. She guessed the door to her left might connect to a bathroom because she caught a hint of tile on the floor at the edge.

She had taken full control of the main door; she considered continuing to attack systems farther into the room and decided against it. Marcant, or someone representing him, had surrendered.

Across the room, partially hidden in shadow, she saw someone sitting still in a chair. The chair was positioned at the center of a mat about four meters on a side. It was a pseudo VR area. The walls were plain as seen through Cilreth's link. She assumed they displayed virtual decoration or data known only to the inhabitant.

Well, these guys are security happy, but they're not killers. As long as they don't think I'm here to kill them...

She let her stealth suit deactivate. Nothing happened, so she took a few steps toward the person. She became paranoid as she crossed the room. She halted, checked the closet opening and the bathroom. She did not see anyone preparing for ambush. Even thoughts of a trap door in the floor came to mind.

What if that's not a person? Or not a live person. Like one of those VRs where the hero discovers a person in a seat facing away from them, and they're dead.

She took two more steps forward as her eyes adjusted. She saw a slender man with white skin and black hair sitting in the control seat. The chair looked highly customized, probably suited to long stints in virtual reality. His eyes were closed and he did not move. His clothes were predictably black, matching the color of his high tech seat.

Not dead... just off-retina.

"Mr. Marcant?" she asked.

The man came back to life. Though he was so pale, he still looked half dead. His ragged hair formed dreadlocks that ended in unimplanted links. It was not currently a popular style, meaning it might be a statement of independence or rebellion. Exactly what it might mean eluded Cilreth, though being older, she was used to many such things going over her head.

"Correct. I am Voss Marcant," he said dramatically. "I'm glad it's you and not Telisa."

"Why?"

"You're the tracker. I wondered if she, then, would be the assassin."

"Assassination is not our intention. Are you really Marcant, or are you the guinea pig Marcant left here to see what's up?" Cilreth said. "Voss. Is that really his first name? He's a Terran male?"

He nodded. "I understand you expect further deception. That's reasonable. Nevertheless, I am Marcant." His eyes narrowed.

I just went up a notch in his book. Or down a notch.

"Well let me get right to it, then. I work for Shiny. Albeit, against my will, half of the time. He has a team of explorers we call PIT. PIT team, the 't' does not stand for team."

Cilreth mentally rolled her eyes at herself. Everyone on Earth now knew what PIT was.

"Anyway, I'm on the PIT team and I'm getting too old for this purple conductive paste, or whatever you guys are calling it these days. So there's a spot on the team opening up."

"You want to hire me?"

"Yes. I'm an expert in Vovokan cybernetics and I can offer that knowledge, as well as the chance to work on a ton of advanced alien hardware and software. In the course of our travels, we investigate many interesting places for Shiny. So there are other alien technologies to find and study. We need help understanding those technologies, typically computer technologies, robots, starship controllers, that sort of thing."

"Intriguing," Marcant said neutrally.

Cilreth looked at his pale skin and glowing blue eyes.

"What are you supposed to be, a vampire? Is that why you're drinking blood?"

Marcant looked at the maroon drink resting in the arm of his seat, almost sorrowful. He answered slowly.

"I'm pale simply because I don't get any light. I drink this beverage because I need—prefer—to replenish blood glucose levels regularly."

Cilreth noticed Marcant looked very slender. She wondered if he had a digestive problem.

"Do you want to apply for the position?"

"Hrm, let's say yes."

I don't think he's serious yet. He will be serious, when he decides I am.

"Do you suffer from limitations that preclude physical activities like, running, jumping, ducking?"

Marcant raised an eyebrow.

"I can do those things. Though not as well as your companion. She seems to run, jump, and duck better than any Terran. Yet she doesn't seem to be a robot. I saw her bleed for a moment."

Ah. So he just wants to learn more.

"She's Trilisk Special Forces. And my boss. That part about Trilisk Special Forces is a joke. Kind of. She lives in an artificial host body, created by Trilisk technology. They wanted to know what it was like to live in other bodies... as long as they remained superior."

"Oh." Marcant lifted an eyebrow again. "Perhaps I could ask questions more directly? Why me?"

"I'm surprised you ask."

"Why are you surprised? It seems a logical question to me," Marcant said.

"I anticipated a narcissist who would just expect everyone to want them. I chose you because of your attempt to crack Shiny's defenses. What was it, the *Thumper*?"

"I'm not familiar with that facility. Or is that an AI?"

"It's Shiny's flagship."

Marcant blinked.

His mind is racing now.

"Look. I said I worked for Shiny, I didn't say I love the golden bastard. And we're offering more than you'll ever find out about Vovokan computers on your own. I chose you because you tried to crack him. You have intelligence and balls. That's a damn good start on being a PIT member right there."

Cilreth got an alert from her link. She was being hacked right now! She checked the services around her: at first, it seemed like a normal dwelling. The many devices all around her offered their services: the table in the far left corner, a cooler by the wall, the waste baskets, and the room thermostat.

Cilreth sent out some counter probes. She found that many of the responses were not standard.

"You're running your own room," Cilreth said. What she meant was that he had altered the software of everything there. And some of it was trying to hack her link.

"Doesn't every self-respecting hacker?" Marcant replied.

"Stop hacking me," Cilreth said calmly.

The attack stopped. "You know, it's illegal to alter your link so that it doesn't obey the standard interface protocol," he said. "I would have succeeded, otherwise."

"*Was* illegal," Cilreth said. "The old world government is defunct. Besides, I doubt you followed those rules even when they were in charge."

Marcant smiled. He threw his hands apart casually. "You caught me," he said.

"You have more questions?" Cilreth asked.

"Yes. Can I bring my girls?"

Cilreth judged his question as disingenuous. She guessed he was just playing around, trying to feel his way through the encounter, or trying to divert her attention...

"If by girls you mean your Skelly scampers, no. We're explorers. We can't take a harem with us." Cilreth answered his question as if it were a serious one.

Marcant shrugged. "No job is perfect."

"I heard you don't mix with your scampers, anyway. I assume you find your jollies virtually. As you say, like every self-respecting hacker."

Marcant nodded. "What alien technologies have you been able to learn about?"

"Vovokan, obviously. To a lesser degree, an advanced race called Celarans. Also a group we call Blackvines. I have samples from machines we called the Destroyers, yeah, great name, I know. They trashed Shiny's homeworld." She paused. "Some Trilisk stuff."

"Trilisk? I doubt it."

Cilreth shrugged. "I haven't programmed anything Trilisk," she admitted. "I think those things are beyond my ability to understand." She had carefully said "my ability", knowing Marcant might rise to the challenge.

He did not ask any other questions, so Cilreth continued.

"Do you oppose Shiny's takeover?" she asked. "You have no chance of stopping him. Even if you're as smart as everyone believes you to be."

"My intelligence is augmented by technology to a greater degree than most others."

"In what ways?"

Please don't say a Trilisk AI.

"There are so many answers. I'm genetically enhanced in ways that are illegal. Were illegal, anyway. Ironically, it was the old government that created me to serve them. They considered themselves above their own laws, of course. So you see I do not oppose Shiny's takeover. I welcome it. For me, it means freedom."

Cthulhu consume us. What if he's a Trilisk? And Telisa's right here. He's toying with us.

"Genetically enhanced? For high intelligence, I suppose. There's a trade off?" She glanced at his drink again. As she asked, Cilreth had her attendants check Marcant for signs of Trilisk presence. He checked clean, so she relaxed.

Marcant touched the edge of his drink cup.

"I need a lot of glucose and a lot of oxygen. What did you do just now?"

"I checked to see if you're a Trilisk. But you're not, and I'm damn happy about it."

Marcant looked impressed.

"Okay so give me another answer," Cilreth prompted.

"I work with machines to enhance my intelligence, of course. We almost all have our links. That's the first step. I'm tightly integrated with more than a link. I also... work with AIs."

"I heard a rumor. You have some AIs?"

"I don't 'have' AIs. I'm friends with a few."

"That doesn't make you smarter."

"It does!" Marcant said emphatically. "I work very synergistically with a couple of them. We become smarter when working together."

Everyone becomes smarter when working on a team. Well, if it's the right team. But I think maybe he means something even more tightly integrated.

Cilreth found Voss Marcant very compelling. She was beginning to see why he had such a following.

"I heard the word symbiote before, when I was investigating you."

Marcant nodded. "That's not going too far. It's an apt word."

"Do you work with a Trilisk? One of your friends, maybe?"

He smiled a creepy smile. At first Cilreth thought he was going to confirm her guess and do something awful.

"No. I believe in them, though. Some don't."

I guess Marcant just has a creepy smile.

"You said you don't oppose Shiny's takeover. Why not?"

"He seems to be a wise, benevolent dictator. And I don't mean that facetiously."

"Seems to be. Why?"

"He gave us our freedoms back. The only crimes left are crimes with victims, where someone is hurt, enslaved, or their property is stolen. His government doesn't even take taxes. It stands on its own."

"And?"

"He removed all forms of super citizenry, except himself. There are no Terran police officers, no judges, no diplomats or lawmakers. Every citizen of Earth stands equal now. He's our leader, and he employs agents, millions of them, but they're machines, not Terrans. They're free of corruption, petty jealousy, ego, everything that always turns our own super citizens against us in tyranny."

"You don't fear that control?"

"No. As he said, actions speak louder than words. He could have exterminated us all by now. He could have forced us to do whatever awful things he wanted. But he didn't do any of that. He lets us live our lives, and so I do trust him. That trust grows every day."

"You're not free to look at his computer systems, though, are you? So you don't know what he's up to."

Marcant shrugged. "They're his. I don't let anyone look at my systems either, if I can help it."

Cilreth felt frustration. How could she explain that Shiny did all those things simply because it was in his best interest at the moment? Or did it matter why he did what he did? Were only the results important?

Shiny can change his mind at any moment and if he does, we might all be in trouble.

"Discuss the possibility that you don't want to oppose Shiny because he's got mind control."

Marcant raised his eyebrows.

"Well, before he ever arrived, I disliked the world government. It's documented. So he did not cause me to hate his predecessors," Marcant began. "If he had mind control, I might forgive him for doing things I would not normally like. So. He took control of the Space Force. Let's suppose I should be angry about that, but I'm not, because he has mind control."

Cilreth nodded. "Yes. Why should we hand the reins of our military over to an alien? You should be set on opposing him at all costs."

"So I should choose the old tyrants over Shiny because he's an alien?"

"Yes. Terrans should run Terra, right? Not an alien."

"The Terrans who ran Earth were greedy, evil bastards."

"Those were Trilisks."

Marcant raised an eyebrow. "Were they all? Really? I've only heard rumors. Shiny hasn't told us much along those lines. If it's all true, doesn't he deserve credit for ousting them and freeing us from their yoke?" Marcant sat forward. "Please, I feel the need to reverse this a moment. Tell me why I should hate him. And I have a feeling you know him much better than I do."

Cilreth let Marcant turn the tables, because she wanted him to know about Shiny.

"Shiny is interested in Shiny. Period. He befriended the PIT team, then betrayed it. If it became advantageous to throw all mankind into incinerators tomorrow, I think he might do it."

"But surely advanced civilizations know that cooperation is superior to competition."

"As long as resources are plentiful and goals are shared, it is. Those circumstances don't always hold."

"Well, Shiny has all the resources he needs. He has the whole solar system. As far as goals, well, he hasn't shared any with us, he lets us pursue our own goals. But with him in control, our goals can't threaten his. So he seems a stable leader, for now."

"For now. That's key. And don't forget that time and attention are resources too, in his mind. He could turn against us even if he has plenty of metal, oxygen, all kinds of materials. If we're slowing him down, distracting him from a goal, I fear that might be enough to make him flip."

"Do you really wonder about the mind control? Or did you just want insight into my thinking?"

"You were caught hacking Vovokan computers. Seems to me like you might be opposing him."

"I'm simply curious. Alien computers—me and my friends are fascinated."

"Then take this job. You'll learn a lot, more than you could ever learn here."

"You know enough about me now? The offer is serious?"

"The offer is serious. Tell me though, are you afraid to take physical risks? Do you have combat skills, incarnate or virtual? Will you travel to other worlds?"

"I can fence," Marcant said. "Not world class, I'm afraid. I've spent my fair share of time living in VRs swinging swords. I do a great Elric... you know, because I'm pale?"

"And skinny."

"Well, yes..."

"And modern arms?"

"Well, they aim and shoot themselves, don't they? Modern arms means assault robots," Marcant said.

"Fair enough. I'll recommend you for the team."

Marcant nodded. "Excellent. I can't wait to meet my new boss."

Chapter 23

The team had started to return to the *New Iridar*. Everyone had obeyed her summons within the ten hours she had given them to arrive. She had left Marcant out of this meeting, even though he had agreed to join the PIT team. Telisa met Imanol as he came on board. Imanol spoke before she could ask a question.

"Shiny caught me. He took the sphere," he admitted.

Telisa sighed. "It's not your fault. Shiny knew I had the cloaking device. He may have anticipated it. What did you find?"

"There's a new facility on that island. But I don't know if the AI is still there."

"I assume he has it. A new facility suggests it might still be there."

"There are the Trilisk tunnels. Maybe he built a research facility to study those. Do you think he uses the AIs for mind control?" Imanol said.

"It's still not clear. We'll all talk about it."

Imanol nodded. "The meeting is soon. I'll clean up quickly."

As Imanol walked away, Telisa considered his report. It seemed like Shiny was ahead at every turn. Telisa sent a message to Cilreth.

"Cilreth. Imanol has been in Shiny's back yard. Keep an eye on him and let me know if anything unusual happens."

"Got it."

Telisa worried about Shiny, Magnus, the new ship, the Space Force ambassador, Marcant, and her current team all in the few minutes before the meeting. By the time she walked into the mess area, she was ready for any distraction.

Telisa saw everyone there, crammed into tiny seats or standing in the corners.

"I've met with Shiny and the Space Force. I don't have an answer about Magnus. What I do have to tell you is that we're getting a better ship. Much more room for everyone."

"How?" asked Cilreth.

"Shiny supplied, just like this one. It will be adapted to Terrans. It's not one of his big ships like the *Clacker*, but a step up nonetheless."

Cilreth rolled her eyes. "Another ship to clean."

"Are you talking about the sand or the software?" Imanol sniped. Telisa ignored it.

"We have an ally in the Space Force. It just so happens, he has a battlecruiser. So he'll be coming with us."

No one knew what to say. Cilreth tried first.

"Why are they coming?"

"They want to send an ambassador to the Celarans, if there are any left. Also, Shiny has told the Space Force about the Destroyers, and equipped the Earth fleet to fight them. At least, to some degree. Since there seems to be a conflict going on between Celarans and Destroyers, maybe we can help."

"Is this battlecruiser going to be more powerful than our ship?" Caden asked.

Telisa raised an eyebrow. "Well, ours is Vovokan. So I think it's at least faster and better defended. I suppose the battlecruiser might outgun us, though."

"What's the name of the Captain? And the ship?"

"Admiral Sager of the *Midway*."

While everyone digested that, Telisa dropped another bomb.

"We also have a new team member coming. You'll find out more about him later. I didn't invite him to this meeting, given its nature."

Telisa sat on one of the tables, then continued. "I want to hear from all of you first. Who wants to report their findings about Earth's change of heart?"

Everyone traded looks until Siobhan spoke. "I'll go."

Telisa watched Siobhan as she gathered herself.

"Earth is nuts. We're famous. Shiny is loved or at least tolerated everywhere. Caden is like a superhero. I'm widely known as the evil woman who 'took him off the market'."

Siobhan shifted in her seat and continued.

"So of course I looked into how fast it happened. It took only about a month. First, everyone assumed the worst. Slowly, reports came in that most of the Space Force had survived intact, where everyone had assumed they had been vaporized in space. Shiny's communication blackout lifted, and suddenly everyone realized most of the people were fine. Then the prisoners of Skyhold came out talking about Trilisks. The Space Force backed up the story. The citizens learned about Shiny and no one knew what to think. Many were preparing for a war of resistance, despite the good news."

"Has Shiny addressed the citizens directly?" asked Imanol.

"Sure. At this point, he made The Shiny Address."

"What!?"

"He announced himself to all of Earth. Look it up," Siobhan said.

Imanol went off retina to investigate. Telisa scanned some clips of it herself. It had happened shortly after the PIT team left on their mission. The most famous piece was:

You see me now as an alien overlord and you are unhappy about it. I understand that. I will prove to you all that you are better off with me in control. I ask the people of Earth to judge me by my actions, not my words.

"This is what he said?" Imanol asked.

"Yes."

"It's not normal Shiny-speak," Telisa pointed out.

"I assume he had it smoothed out to normal sounding Terran, given the occasion. Then he started taking action. More action than anyone thought possible. More action than the world government had taken in all the years of its existence."

"Well what did he do first?" Imanol asked.

"Removed all VR quotas. Well, that's the big thing from the start that everyone remembers," Siobhan said.

"How does it work with unlimited VR quota? Why does anyone ever come out?" Imanol asked.

"Well you need to come out once a week just to do some basic body maintenance, you know? Shiny hasn't gotten all the bugs worked out yet. You still need to get up, walk around some, take a toning pill and some vitamin balancers. Something too about being conscious for a few minutes every week to keep your muscles connected to your brain. I can't remember exactly. But Shiny made that easy, too!"

"How?"

"He improved the incarnate activities available," Jason said. "There are a bunch of incarnate parties and special events going on all the time. It's a blast to actually get out once a week and see your friends, you know, face to face. Everyone takes that time to eat some real food and share stories about their virtual adventures."

"It's our natural evolution," Cilreth said. "That's how it went on Vovok, too, you know. It's inevitable for virtual reality to eventually supersede reality."

Supersede, ha, Telisa thought.

"Well, who goes in and fixes things when stuff goes all conductive purple?" Imanol asked.

"Shiny fixes it. I mean, not personally, but you know. Vovokan stuff fixes anything that breaks."

"Of course he does," Imanol said. "With everyone off in imaginary worlds, he's free to do whatever he wants. Less people watching him, questioning him."

"Maybe true," Siobhan said. "But he's not making anyone do it. Core World citizens just love it. Reality is too dangerous and boring for them."

"Because they don't do anything meaningful," Caden mumbled.

"Says the Blood Glades champ?" Imanol said.

"Next time we're in a fight and I save your ass—"

"On topic, please," Telisa said. "What next?"

"Well everyone talked about him for weeks. They wanted to know more about him. They gathered information and rumors and circulated it all to death, until everyone decided they loved him. Then they went back to their entertainments."

Siobhan's flow of information stopped. She looked at Telisa, who decided Siobhan was done.

"Caden?" Telisa prompted.

"I talked with my parents and many others, rather than relying on the network," Jason said. "Siobhan and I decided we would each take a different approach for more varied results."

Telisa nodded.

"Earth loves Shiny because he's been a good to Earth," Caden said.

"Because of his actions?" Cilreth asked.

"That's just it. He actually did what everyone wanted."

"He can't have made everyone happy. You know how that goes," Cilreth said.

"Well, that's true, but he went further than anyone else ever got," Caden said. "He took a long list of demands from citizens and organizations and implemented them."

"Examples?"

"There are several societies that lamented the extinction of most of Earth's natural animal species. As you know, at the end we pretty much just took DNA samples and let everything slide. We all told ourselves we'll recreate the wild again someday when we have the technology and resources. Well, that never really happened with the UN in charge. And of course, once the arms buildup started, we never looked back. Well, Shiny created dozens of huge islands out in the ocean and populated them with extinct species. He did such a good job of it, the ecosystems actually work. There are drones out there for people to interface with that don't bother the animals at all. People can see the wildlife anytime they want."

"Well, there's no way he could have accomplished everything on the list... is there?" Telisa asked.

"You're right, there's a long tail of requests. Impossibly long. But he's made his way so far down it, that 99.9% of the world's population are totally satisfied. He met some esoteric demands. Some society wanted 100,000 of Earth's top historic sites restored and maintained just as they had been in antiquity. I mean everything from Pompeii to the library at Alexandria, the Greek temples, Stonehenge, the list went on and on. Shiny didn't restore the sites—but he created virtual realities containing the entire list. He incorporated some amazing research and technologies that have made the VR sites so authentic the society realized it's better than anything they had asked for. He even inhabited the sites with artificial denizens that live out their lives in the way we believe they did in the past. Anyone can visit these virtual realities and they can even choose the time they want to visit and it's all there, to a level of detail that astounds them."

"Sound familiar?" Cilreth said.

"It makes me think of Trilisks living in alien bodies, hidden among the populace," Telisa said.

"Well, those people aren't real, and—"

"Yes. Still, that thought crossed my mind."

Jason looked hesitant, but Telisa could tell he wanted to say something.

"What do you think, Jason?" Telisa asked.

"I think we've been thinking too small," Jason said. "Mind control is too small. This is Trilisk technology we're talking about. The prayers we used were just our primitive way with interacting with it. I think Shiny's taken it to the next level."

"Explain," Telisa said. He had her full attention.

"I've noticed that more things are consistently happening that make people happy," Jason said. "I think the AI uses resources to see what's going on inside people's heads, then engineers happiness from the outside."

"So I guess Caden wanted to be famous?" Imanol spat.

"He wanted to be exonerated publicly," Telisa said, before Siobhan and Caden could get bent out of shape.

"But Siobhan is..." Caden stopped.

"Yes?" Telisa prompted. "Are you happy with recent events, Siobhan?"

Siobhan nodded. "Oddly, I am. No corporate assassins came for me, and I'm widely envied."

Cilreth found what she was looking for. And Marcant is getting what he wants. To study alien technology.

Telisa made the next leap by thinking about what she wanted. Her breath caught.

Then I might get Magnus back?

She immediately clamped down on the rising hope and tried to keep it small. Jason was just theorizing. Telisa's emotions were too flustered to speak about it with everyone, so she moved things on before anyone asked about her.

"I no longer think Shiny is controlling everyone," Telisa said.

Imanol's mouth opened but he could not say anything. Before he finally expressed his ridicule, Siobhan spoke up.

"She's right. It's sad, but the Earthers just don't care who's in charge as long as they're not bored. And Shiny caused a revolution in VR entertainment and increased everyone's VR time half again. Between all the new automation and the Trilisk AIs, Earth has nothing to do but live their whole lives in VR. They're happy, and as long as they're happy, they don't care who's in charge out here in reality."

"But there were protests, underground resistance organizations—"

"And they evaporated. The ones left are people who were in charge before just for the ego trip and now Shiny doesn't need them. Only a tiny fraction of the population is gunning for a new world order. And they're widely hated for it, because they sabotage the VR network and go into people's homes to disconnect their life support. Those robots we called Shiny's enforcers when we arrived are out protecting people in VR. They aren't oppressing anyone except the saboteurs."

"Is this what Earth comes to? Just a bunch of people wired into VR their whole lives?" Imanol asked.

"Maybe that's what becomes of Earth, but it doesn't have to be what becomes of humanity," Caden said. "We can recruit the ones who crave real adventure and take them to the frontier. Or we can just recruit from the frontier. Let Earth do what it wants."

"They may be doing what they want now, but if they don't resist Shiny..."

"Then what? Shiny already has complete control," Telisa said. "Whatever nefarious plan he has, there's no reason to wait on it. He would have revealed it by now. Turns out, a benevolent dictator can be a good thing."

"What about the Space Force?" Imanol asked. "They don't spend every waking hour in VR."

"The Space Force people have kept the illusion of control over their affairs and they have more ships and machines than ever before," Caden said. "They're happy for other reasons. At least they're ready to help us with the Celarans."

"Go gather your things. We'll move to the new ship as soon as it shows up, which could be anytime now. Our new team member will meet us there."

"Who is it?" asked Caden.

"Just meet him and ask," Telisa dodged.

Imanol and Cilreth left so quickly she almost wondered if they were hooking up for a moment, until she dismissed the idea, knowing Cilreth's preferences. Jason left more slowly. Telisa was surprised and impressed with his report.

If he's onto something real, he uncovered more than anyone else. Although Cilreth and Imanol sure had a lot more on their plate than the others.

Caden and Siobhan had not moved from their spot leaning against a food machine. Telisa listened to them with her sharpened hearing as she walked away.

"What do you think about a new team member?" Caden asked.

"I'll be slow to trust them, whoever it is," Siobhan said.

"Can we trust anyone from Earth?"

"You mean the mind control theory?"

"Do you ever wonder about it?" Caden asked.

"What? You mean, if it is mind control and..."

"And it worked on us, too."

"All the time," Siobhan said.

***

"I didn't ask you what you found out," Telisa said to Cilreth. They were in Cilreth's quarters. Telisa could barely fit in because Cilreth had a large, comfortable chair centrally located for her off-retina work. Cilreth worked to dismantle the assembly as they talked.

"I was distracted. But everyone seemed happy. Even me."

"We could never imagine what life would be like with something like the Trilisk AI around. The Trilisks really were ridiculously farther along than we are. It's scary to think anything could topple them."

"Methane-breathers. That's all we really know, right?"

Telisa shrugged. "Nothing, for sure."

"So Marcant accepted?" Cilreth asked. Telisa decided the question was simply an information prompt, since Telisa had already announced he would join the team.

"Yes, he's on the team. I've arranged for him to meet us on the new ship. Are you coming on the next expedition?"

"Yes. One more," Cilreth said. "Safe duty on the ship again, I hope. Though Marcant isn't exactly a land warrior himself."

"He goes by Marcant, not Voss?"

"He's known among his followers as Marcant. That's what he prefers."

"So I assume from his reputation, he'll be up to speed quickly?"

Cilreth took a moment to respond.

"Here's what you need to keep in mind about Marcant. He's not one person, he's three. He works closely with two AIs. Which means of the three, the one you see is the dumbest. If those three work with us, they'll be invaluable."

"But if they decide to cross purposes with us, then it'll be like Shiny all over again," Telisa said.

"I think he's worth the risk. He's a Terran. I hope we can earn loyalty or at least understand each other better."

"Probably."

"Another plus, he said he hacked Shiny out of curiosity, but I think he wanted to work against Shiny. He's just afraid to admit it to us. Which is only smart."

Telisa nodded.

"Good. Get yourself moved over with the others," Telisa told her. "Shiny has summoned me to give his answer to my proposal."

Cilreth hugged Telisa. "No matter what, don't give up."

"I won't."

Michael McCloskey

Chapter 24

The new ship had two mess halls, and each one was the size of the Vovokan scout vessel they had used on the last mission. Jason explored the ship with Siobhan and Caden. They left the galley and headed down a wide corridor. It looked just like the hallway on a Terran passenger ship, right down to the maroon carpet and elegant glow rods.

"Did you think about staying on Earth, Jason?" Siobhan asked.

"For a little while. But being on this team is like being a VR star, except for real."

"I choose the real thing, too, even though it will end me sooner or later," Caden said. He stopped to check out a bathroom on the corridor they walked down.

"Oh the luxury," he said. "No sand in my toilet! I think I'm gonna cry!""

"I bet when you flush it still goes into a sand cleaner," Siobhan said. "The inside looks Terran but it's all Vovokan under the covers."

"Shhh, don't ruin it for me," Caden replied.

"It's nice here, but remember the *Clacker* when we could pray up anything?" Siobhan said.

Caden rolled his eyes. "Forever spoiled!"

Jason did not smile, though he was as happy as anyone else with Shiny's latest gift. Supposedly it had been created just for the PIT team. Cilreth had said it was designed from the ground up for Terrans, but it used Vovokan technology, making it better than any Terran ship yet built.

"Why is doing something for real more satisfying?" Jason asked.

"It's harder. More dangerous. And the girls love daredevils," Caden said, looking at Siobhan. She did not fall for his bait.

"I think it's because it's fleeting. What you've achieved, you can lose," she said. "You can't just save the state of the world and keep it that way forever. And you can't go back and undo your mistakes."

They entered a large bay. The walls extended outwards from the silvery metal floor in a bulging convex shape. Jason's first thought was that their old ship could fit into the wide open space.

"Frackjammers!" Siobhan said.

Jason followed Siobhan's gaze. There in the side of the bay, he saw them: four Vovokan battle spheres. They sat quiescent, nestled in a row against the wall.

"Spawn of—" he started.

"We've been escalated," Caden said sullenly.

"What's wrong?" a new voice said.

Jason turned. A strange man stood a few meters away. Jason found his right hand on his stunner. He was the most reserved of his group. Caden and Siobhan already brandished drawn weapons.

The man stood very still. Jason found him extremely slender and pale. He wore black clothing as if trying to contrast his pallor. Jason found the stranger's long face neither handsome nor ugly.

"Hi, I'm Jason," he said.

The pale man dipped his head a bit. "Marcant."

Jason forgot all about his weapon. "*The* Marcant? Wow, great to meet you!"

Marcant's mouth turned up just a bit on one end. He nodded. "The same. You made a splash at Stark's."

"Who is he?" Siobhan asked.

"He's a famous... freedom worker. And our new team member, no doubt," Jason said.

"Freedom worker?" asked Siobhan.

"Of the cagey software insinuation kind," Caden said. "Though a lot of people doubt your existence."

"You saw me at Stark's?" Jason blurted.

"I must admit I wasn't watching at the time," Marcant said. "But the moment has been celebrated by many once they learned you were somehow associated with PIT. I thought perhaps you were simply a front man for the business, but I see from your Veer suit here you're a real team member."

"We'll get you in one yourself in no time," Caden said. "We can use a wizard like you on the team. We get more than our fair share of cryptic alien stuff to figure out."

"I'm certain you will," Marcant said neutrally. Jason could not tell if he spoke of the Veer armor, the alien tech, or both.

Caden and Siobhan lowered their weapons, though they did not put them away. Jason smiled, trying to show Marcant at least one friendly face. Being the newest member of the team, he remembered the challenge of fitting in.

"You're unhappy about those devices over there? What are they, nuclear weapons?" Marcant asked.

Jason glanced back at the spheres. "Vovokan battle spheres. War machines," he said.

"They're not yours?"

"Oh, they're *ours* alright," Caden said. "Our watchdogs."

"They're kind of to keep us in line, or at least we assume that," Jason said.

Marcant frowned. "I have authority to order them," he said. "Dare I?

Jason checked with his own link. The machines offered him link services. "I guess we do."

One of the spheres lifted a meter off the ground. Another one rolled forward like a giant bowling ball as they tested out their control.

"Well, that's nice, but we know who really controls them when it counts," Siobhan said.

"I'll see what I can do about that," Marcant said. His voice spoke of rising to a challenge.

Could Marcant really do that? Could he really hack Shiny's battle spheres? Jason wondered.

"I wish you luck," Jason said.

Marcant raised a gray sphere in one hand. "I have a sphere, too," he said.

Siobhan had her laser pistol trained on Marcant in a split second.

"Hold! I was told to return this," Marcant said quickly. It was the first break of his unnatural calm that Jason had noticed.

"That's Telisa's cloaking sphere. What're you doing with it?" asked Caden.

"Shiny told me to give it to Telisa."

"You spoke with him?" asked Jason.

"What was he doing with it?" Siobhan asked at the same time.

Marcant decided to answer both questions at once. "He did not say how he came to have it during our brief audience."

"Has he done something to her? If that bug thinks we're going to work for him without Telisa, he's got another thing coming," Caden said.

Marcant raised an eyebrow. "Telisa is on her way, at least according to a shuttle passenger list," he said.

The others paused as they tried to verify that off-retina. Jason himself finally found it.

"You're on the ball. That's good, we can use someone like you," Jason said. "I take it you're going to work with Cilreth."

"I'm supposed to work with you all. A full-fledged member of PIT, I'm told."

"Is this Shiny's doing?" Siobhan asked. She looked at Marcant. Jason detected a hint of malice.

"You don't trust me. I get it. Maybe when Telisa arrives, she can verify what is and isn't Shiny's doing."

"What did Shiny say to you?" Jason asked.

"He said that I wanted to learn about alien technology, and that I would get what I wanted."

"A lot of that going around lately," Siobhan said. Marcant gave her a puzzled look.

"We believe the Trilisk AIs are making things happen that satiate the populace," Jason explained.

"Trilisk AIs? Plural?" Marcant looked fascinated.

Suddenly Jason realized that Telisa did not necessarily want to share that information with the newest member of the team. His glance to Caden and Siobhan verified it: they stared back at him rather coldly.

"Telisa can catch you up on that," Caden said. His tone indicated he wanted that conversational thread to hold there.

"Your secrets are limitless. You said this sphere is a cloaking device?"

"Yes. Alien."

"Which race of aliens?"

"I don't know," Jason said. He looked at Caden.

"Telisa found it in Shiny's vault on Vovok. I don't know what race created it either," Caden said. He seemed to be returning to his good mood.

"This ship gets my seal of approval," Caden continued. "What should we call this thing?"

"*Newer Iridar*," Siobhan immediately suggested.

"We can only take that purple paste so far," Jason said. "Might as well just go for *Iridar III*."

"*Iridar*," said Telisa's voice. She walked in from a door ten meters from the group. "Whatever ship we're using, it's just *Iridar*."

Something was off. Telisa looked *wrong*. Jason figured it out quickly.

She's smiling!

"Something good?" Siobhan said, clearly just as intrigued as Jason.

"Someone has something for me?" Telisa asked, walking up to Marcant.

Marcant held the small metal ball up in his hand. Telisa accepted it. "I got my stealth sphere back."

Jason nodded. Something was still off. Telisa still grinned like an idiot.

Oh no. Did Shiny get to her too?

"Oh yeah. And we got him," she said, pointing a thumb over her shoulder. Her smile grew even wider. Jason saw Magnus step out of a doorway behind her.

"I'm back," Magnus said.

Chapter 25

Telisa met Marcant in the main room of his personal quarters on the *Iridar*. Marcant had been led to understand these new spaces were larger than what the team had taken out on their last mission. It was an order of magnitude smaller than Marcant's own sanctuary, but he had expected that. Adair had summed it up: the quarters were adequate.

He sat on one of the five black lounges that furnished the room along a long, curved wall. A narrow walkway behind the lounges allowed Marcant to pace back and forth which served him well. He liked to pace. Marcant had littered the flat anchor points here and there with his usual off-retina public feeds from Earth. He preferred to keep his more private research in the viewpanes of his internal PV. He allowed Telisa to see the public feeds as well, so the room would not seem dark and cold.

When Telisa walked in, Marcant went on-retina and faced her.

"I'm pleased to see you on board," Telisa said. "Are you finding these accommodations cramped?"

"About what I expected," he said. "I'm pleased to find that it's Vovokan, however. Cilreth has started my studies in that direction."

"Good. Just don't take over the ship and crash it."

Marcant smiled, though Telisa said it as if it was not a joke.

"I promise to be careful."

"And your AI friends? Are you in contact with them? Will they by chance be going?" she said.

"Yes," he said. He reached into his black suit and pulled out the two AI cores. "Adair and Achaius."

Telisa looked at them with interest. "They don't want bodies of their own?" Telisa asked.

No doubt Cilreth filled her in regarding my eccentricities.

"I hear we have some robots on board," Marcant said.

"Yes..." Telisa said. She made the obvious assumption. "They can each use one of those, if they wish. I'm not sure Shiny—"

"I'll tell them to avoid the Vovokan battle spheres," Marcant offered. "Besides, even though there is an interface to command them, it's not quite at the low level that an AI would want to control everything."

"Yes, I assume the battle spheres had minds of their own. I don't know how smart they are, though."

"I'm glad to meet with you incarnate. I was hoping to ask you some questions too," Marcant said.

"Sure. What would you like to talk about?" Telisa asked as she slipped down onto one of the lounges. Marcant was struck again by her charisma, but Adair snapped him back to focus.

"Ask her about what she is," Achaius said to Marcant privately. "We can learn more details than what Cilreth told us."

"Yes, play ignorant," Adair agreed. "Let's hear it from her."

"Your team is very talented," Marcant said to Telisa. "Cilreth handles herself well, and from what I understand, combat isn't at all her strong point. You on the other hand... how did you do all those things, when you visited the sanctuary?"

"'Visited'. Hah," Adair mumbled to Marcant. "So diplomatic of you." Marcant ignored it.

"Alien technology," Telisa said. "I'm enhanced. Shiny has arranged for me to operate in an artificial body."

"So you're Vovokan tech?"

Telisa's mouth twitched. "Trilisk, actually."

Marcant sat up even further. "How is that possible?"

"Shiny has come across some real gems in his pursuit of Trilisk artifacts. And we found more pursuing some remnants of their race here and there."

"Such as Trilisk AIs?"

Telisa hesitated a second.

"Oops! Delicate subject," Adair announced in Marcant's head.

"Now we'll see how much she trusts us," Achaius added.

"Yes, he has one or two," Telisa finally said. "They're extremely powerful artifacts, capable of feats which seem magical to primitive races like us Terrans."

"Se he... keeps those under wraps?"

"Very much so. I'm sorry. I would love to spend my life studying one," Telisa said.

Marcant decided to move on.

"Who else has an advanced body like you? Magnus? Caden?"

"It's only me. Shiny's way of cementing my leadership, playing on Terran instincts to follow the strongest, I think."

"Well then he should have made you a foot taller and given you bulging muscles. The appearance of strength might play into instincts just as well, if not more than, your actual strength."

Telisa smiled. "We're in agreement. I think he may have missed a nuance there, given us too much credit. But Shiny does what Shiny does."

"What's the deal with him? He's running this game, really, isn't he?"

"For now," Telisa said in a voice loaded with meaning. "He's doing a good job, it seems."

"I don't know how to probe that subject further," Marcant said privately to Achaius and Adair.

"Neither do I," Adair said. "What about the rest of the team?"

"Where are the others?" Marcant asked Telisa.

"What others?" Telisa asked.

Marcant cleared his throat. "Parker, Haist, Arakaki, Kirilenko... Captain Relachik?"

"Dead," Telisa said forcefully in a flat voice.

Marcant watched her. She did not seem angry at him for asking.

"Is she going to offer details?" Adair asked Marcant on the private channel with Achaius.

Telisa decided to continue. "Killed by aliens. Shiny got some of them, and others fell fighting Trilisks. Did Cilreth make clear that being on our team carries such risks?"

"Downplayed it a bit," Marcant said.

"Well we haven't left Earth yet," Telisa said, stating the obvious. She piped through an external feed. The dark, curved wall before them flickered to life. It showed a view of Earth from space. The glowing blue orb was huge in the room, as wide as two of the lounges. Marcant stared at it. He had seen such scenes many times before. The difference was, this time, it was real, and he contemplated leaving that huge blue ball.

"You have a couple of hours to change your mind. After that, I want you all in. We'll start your training. We won't put you into a real situation you can't handle, if we can help it. Of course, unexpected things happen on the frontier, or beyond it, so you have to consider the risk."

"Another question?"

"Yes, ask more."

"Why do you do it?"

"I started out to satisfy my own curiosity about the universe," she said. Telisa looked off-retina, but Marcant supposed perhaps she was simply thinking this time. "Now, I see more than that. We have a duty to our race. Terrans won't be just digging around in alien ruins for much longer. There are aliens we need to make friends with, and aliens we need to prepare to fight against. We have to learn as much as we can."

"Who gets to keep the artifacts?"

"Shiny will want the biggest and best. For the most part, he only needs one example of anything though. He has ways of making more. Otherwise, I lean toward letting you keep things. I suppose I would ask for something you found if the whole team could benefit greatly for sharing it."

Marcant nodded. "I understand. I'm mostly in it for what I can learn, anyway."

Telisa stood. "You'll be able to learn a lot. We have no shortage of mysteries and alien systems to analyze. Send me any other questions you have. I'm going to make my last preparations."

"Thank you... do you have a title if I join?"

"No. It's just Telisa, whether you join us or not." She walked out. Marcant stared at the huge display. He took Adair and Achaius out to stare at them. The silver spheres had a slight blue and red tint, respectively. They each held a mind as powerful as his own, wholly dedicated to his success. They were his family.

"This is too dangerous," Adair said. "I can't protect you out there."

"The rewards are huge," Achaius said. "We've learned more about Vovokan technology in the last day than we learned in years previously."

"I can grub around, spending months planning attempts to get into Shiny's networks just to fail over and over, or I can join this team. This is the way forward. At least for now, we need to do this," Marcant said.

"For healthy self interest," Achaius said.

"That part about keeping Earth safe was compelling," Adair said, sounding a bit miffed.

Marcant had already mostly made up his mind; he would not pull out now. Unlike most people, he had no trouble with big decisions. The challenge was making the best of the decisions that had been made.

"So, about the robotic bodies," Marcant said.

"Yes? You have something in mind?"

"How about those attendants, for starters," Marcant said. "Cilreth has learned a lot about them. You could each have more than one."

"Today the tiny spheres... tomorrow, those big ones in the bay," Achaius said.

"For once, we are agreed, Achaius," Adair said.

Chapter 26

Magnus stood next to Telisa in the cargo bay. Cilreth sat on a cargo container across from them, and Imanol paced on his right. Magnus asked for news in bits and pieces, trying to let himself absorb everything slowly.

"The Space Force ship *Midway* is going out with us on this one, as well as one of Shiny's battleships," Cilreth said.

Magnus shook his head. It was so much to take in.

"Give it time, you'll be up and running with us just like before," Cilreth said to him.

Imanol smiled. "She's right. But don't listen to Twitch Queen if she says you need a little boost to get through it."

Magnus stared at Imanol blankly.

"He likes to make pet names for us and pretend he's a grumpy old man," Cilreth said. "Which is dumb, because I've already got grumpy old woman down cold."

"What's his name for me?" Magnus asked Cilreth on the private channel.

"It varies. Last I heard, he called you 'The Machine'," Cilreth said. "He calls Telisa 'Trilisk Special Forces'. I think he gives the good names to everyone he's afraid of pissing off."

Magnus smiled. It felt good to smile.

These people are tight. Like family. Imanol is older and wiser than the others. I guess he's joined the old timers' council.

Magnus no longer felt like part of the family. Worse, he had identified an irrational sense of resentment in himself. Telisa had gone on with her life without him. He had been left behind, and now everything had changed.

Blame Shiny. It's not her fault!

Magnus hated it when his emotions refused to toe the line of intellect. He took a deep breath and resolved to give it time as Cilreth had suggested.

"Siobhan made some advancements on your robot designs," Telisa said. "Just tweaks here and there. She's a good engineer, and not half bad at hacking either."

"So we use a lot of attendants too? How many robots?"

"Yes we have a lot of attendants, and those are our primary scouts. As for your robots, that's up to you and Siobhan. Make lots, is my feeling," Telisa said.

"Make the soldier ones, please," Imanol said. "And the carrier mules. The attendants should always work best for scouting."

Magnus nodded. "Soldiers and carriers. Will do."

"We can't pray them up anymore," Telisa said.

"That's okay. I look forward to it, the old fashioned way."

No one said anything for a moment, so Magnus decided to learn about the new guy.

"So Marcant is some kind of genius? He can figure out alien artifacts?"

"He's not one of us," Imanol said. "He doesn't act like it. He's self absorbed."

"Fast conclusions! He's been on the team for what, a day now?" Telisa asked.

"He's smart and he has smart AIs. His hacker approach is exactly what's needed. Remember, I'm supposed to be a people finder," Cilreth said.

"He's curious. That'll hook him once he gets a taste," Telisa said. Magnus nodded. If Marcant had the bug like Telisa did, it would happen just like she said. She caught his eye and smiled.

"We're going to sleep," Telisa announced. It sounded like a proclamation. Magnus saw Imanol smile. Magnus half expected a crack about their early turn in, but Imanol said nothing.

Telisa and Magnus left and walked to her quarters. She lived in a large stateroom, at least 12 meters on a side. The large space held no decorations. To Magnus it felt almost sad. He saw a collection of weapons hanging on the wall next to three Veer suits. Some of them had holes and bloodstains. Deactivated attendants sat on the floor in every nook. A large sleep net had been deployed across a corner.

Telisa towed Magnus to her sleep net eagerly. She smiled and flung herself across him. Magnus responded to her, yet something was wrong. He tried to aggressively pursue their physical reunion, ignoring some ache in his psyche. Telisa broke away.

"What's wrong?" she said.

"I'm a little weirded out," he said stiffly. "Everything will be fine once I've found my new place, and familiarized myself with everyone again. I need to make up for lost time."

"Your new place? Magnus. I worked hard to get you back. Your place here isn't new. It's the same as it was when Shiny took you. And I haven't been close to anyone else since you were taken from me."

"I believe you. I just need to catch up."

"That's what we're doing now," Telisa said, and kissed him again, more slowly. "Relax. In a week it'll feel like you were here all along, I promise."

Magnus kissed her back and forgot about his worries.

***

"You're different."

Magnus said it gently. They had been in her room sleeping on and off for about six hours.

"I was afraid you'd say that," she said.

"It's not bad. You have less heart, and your eyes are harder now. You've done an amazing job leading the team. The changes are inevitable. You make decisions, take the consequences onto your shoulders... it changes a person."

Telisa slid an arm behind his neck and squeezed. Magnus felt the immense strength in her slender arm. He laughed.

"Yes, and your body's harder, too."

"Trilisk Special Forces. That's what Imanol called it."

Magnus smiled. He felt a spike of jealousy but did not let it show.

I should have been here too. Damn you Shiny.

"I'm proud of you. And so glad to be back."

"You'll always be my teacher. My life teacher," Telisa said. "Shiny gave me the job but I need your help."

"You have it, not that you need it."

"Let's roll!"

Magnus laughed. They dove out of the sleeping web onto the floor. The surface was firm but not hard. Just about right for some Jiu Jitsu.

A long arm extended from the wall and dropped off a thick top and a pair of rugged pants for Telisa. She slipped into them. Magnus looked around and decided he did not have anything to wear except his Veer suit.

"It's okay," Telisa said. "It's either that, or some paper clothes." She laughed. He joined her.

"I'll never wear any of that Core World disposable crap."

"I know," she said.

When he was in his suit, they grasped onto each other, looking for a leverage advantage. They alternately pushed and pulled, trying to out-time the other. Magnus pushed a bit harder, testing her strength again. She matched him.

Her resistance reversed in an instant. Magnus fell forward despite being ready for her move. Telisa's leg extended, pulling him the rest of the way forward with inexorable force. Then she used her right arm, hooked under his left, to flip him. He slid forward onto his back while she placed her weight squarely above him.

She twirled to a new mount and went for his arm, holding it in her hands and sweeping a leg around until she had the arm isolated. Magnus turned, pulling his elbow back through the danger zone. He tried to take advantage of the failed armbar and pass her guard around the back, but she moved too quickly. He found her shin before his chest, blocking him, then in a lightning motion it had slipped over his arm and wrapped around his neck. Her other leg locked it under his right arm. He braced his right hand against his head and grabbed his own collar, but Telisa's arm ripped it away. The pressure increased until he tapped her side with his left arm.

"Good one. You're better!" he said.

"I wish I could say it was all skill," she said. "I've been training, but obviously it's my new body, too."

Magnus smiled.

"It's good for me. I was getting by with you on strength now and then, being lazy. Now that you're stronger, I'll be forced to perfect my technique."

She smiled. "Your techniques are already perfect," she said, glancing back at the sleep web.

"You miss me? To me it seems like it was just yesterday that we—" he shrugged.

"See, maybe you had it the easiest of the two of us," Telisa said.

"So Caden and Siobhan are a thing."

"Oh, you noticed that?" Telisa said coyly. "Go ahead... say something about that."

Magnus knew what she meant. How could he express any concern about Caden and Siobhan's arrangement when it was exactly that Magnus and Telisa were doing?

"Again?" he asked.

"The web or the roll?"

"Yes."

"You got it."

***

Magnus faced Marcant on an empty plain of gently waving grass. They circled each other two meters apart, each holding a thin, light sword. They wore modern Veer armor which clashed with the primitive weaponry.

"Swords? I'm surprised," Marcant said, raising his light weapon and keeping it between them as they moved. The point of his double-edged sword remained aimed at Magnus's face.

"You said you fence. I know these aren't quite rapiers, but..."

"Ah, yes, I participate in the occasional virtual fantasy battle," Marcant said. He thrust at Magnus, who deflected the thrust and riposted. Marcant stopped and resumed his circle. Then he tested Magnus again, this time thrusting several times as Magnus replied. Magnus's weapon moved a bit more out of line than Marcant's. Magnus took a step back.

Marcant changed his sword's position and thrust low. Magnus moved away, then batted aside the second thrust and counter-attacked. Marcant started to move straight back, then suddenly circled instead. Magnus reacted smoothly.

Marcant smiled. His breath now came in rapid gasps, but he pressed again. This time he kept thrusting and countering in a long sequence until Magnus's weapon came too far off line. Finally a thrust made it through, striking Magnus in the collar of his Veer suit, directly into the front of his throat.

"Aha!" Marcant said. "I got you!"

"Good job," Magnus said calmly. Unlike Marcant, he was not breathing hard; the virtual environment took their actual physiques into account.

Marcant smiled. "This is most unexpected! I know this is only swordplay, not modern weapons, but at least I have one specialty that..." he trailed off. Magnus just stared at him.

"That's not your dominant hand, is it?" Marcant asked.

Magnus shook his head.

"Of course not," Marcant said, deflated. "What shall we do now?"

"Now I'll take you through a series of modern weapons training," Magnus said. "Just the basics so that you wouldn't hurt yourself in real life if you were to pick one up. Then you start training with the team."

"Really? So soon? Won't they... will I slow them down?"

"Most likely. But you will in real life, too, so they should do virtual training with you so they're used to picking up your slack. You should also take something to increase your lung capacity and integrate some incarnate physical training."

"You're not happy about this, are you?" Marcant asked.

Magnus raised a hand as if apologizing for a bad tennis serve.

"I'm fine with it. All I want is for you to apply that formidable intelligence of yours to the combat studies. Learn and improve. I understand this is not your strong point; combat skill is not why Cilreth and Telisa have added you to the team."

Marcant nodded. The sword in his hand became a laser rifle.

"Here we go," Magnus said.

***

Two days later, Magnus observed Marcant's first virtual outing with the rest of the team. Magnus stood in an empty room, doing a light workout as he watched in his

PV. The team walked on an alien planet, looking for an artifact.

"I don't think this deployment is optimum," Marcant said. "Our heavy hitters are on point with us trailing behind. Instead, when the attendants find a threat, then Magnus, Caden, and Telisa should deploy against it once we know what and where it is, with the rest of us to protect their flanks, or even flank the enemy."

"They're on point because they have the most experience," Imanol said.

"Maybe they have the most experience because they're always on point," Marcant said to Imanol.

"In training, we usually all rotate," Imanol said. "They have the most real world experience. Right now, we're doing this to get you used to what will likely happen in the real world, sometime soon."

"Imanol's right," Siobhan said.

"Let me demonstrate it to you," Marcant said. "Caden, you fall back to the middle—"

"Not this time. When you're the designated leader show us what you have. Until then, obey your orders," Jason said.

"How's he doing?" Telisa said aloud. Magnus brought his focus back on-retina and turned to regard her. He had not heard her enter.

"Having trouble integrating. He wants a leadership role before he's established himself."

"I'll have a talk with him," she said.

"For all I know, he may well have good input to provide," Magnus said, hedging a bit. "But he needs to be sensitive about when his ideas will be accepted by the others."

"Got it."

Telisa stayed with Magnus to watch the outcome. The team managed to obtain the target artifact and return without losing anyone. Marcant seemed to have decided to stop trying to interact and just get the mission over with.

"He's slogging it now," Magnus said.

"Right, anything to get it over with," Telisa agreed. The simulation ended.

Telisa wasted no time. She went into the room where everyone had linked in and walked up to Marcant. She offered Magnus a feed of her hearing and vision. He took it and brought it up in a pane in his PV.

This should be interesting, Magnus thought.

"Marcant, with me," Telisa said. She said it mildly, sending the signal to everyone that he was not being punished.

Marcant nodded and followed Telisa into an empty stateroom.

"I can tell you have a good grasp of strategy and tactics," Telisa said, as the door closed. Magnus saw her vision turn to regard Marcant.

"Well it's actually my friend, Achaius. Anyway, if you can see that, then why did everyone back blockhead back there?"

"Imanol? He's not a blockhead. He just doesn't accept newcomers quickly. You need their respect first," Telisa said. "What good is your superior insight and ability if no one listens to you?"

"Well, they should be smart enough to listen to good advice," Marcant said carefully.

"I can tell you're going to be our tactician someday," Telisa said.

"Really? I mean, I know I can do it, but I'm surprised you see that."

"Here's what you do. Be humble. Accept their crap for a while, build up your respect bank with them. Show them what you can do for a while. They'll come to accept you. When you're at that spot, I'll put you in charge for several training scenarios. Then, when they see how much ass you kick, they'll realize you were right all along. Then, Magnus and I will put you in charge of more and more. Sound reasonable?"

Magnus and I. Did she say that because I'm listening?

"Eminently," Marcant said, straightening in his seat.

"Imanol may bait you. Ignore it for now, until you see the lay of the land... meaning the way they relate to each other."

Marcant nodded.

"Okay, I'll talk to you later," Telisa said.

Cilreth walked into Magnus's room before Telisa came back. Magnus turned to meet her. Imanol was on her heels.

"Can you believe this guy?" asked Imanol. "Did you see all that?"

Magnus shrugged. He let his reply drag until Telisa came back and told the door to close behind her.

"He's trouble," Imanol persisted.

"We're going to keep an eye on him," Telisa said.

"So you agree?"

Cilreth looked pensive. "He's good. We know that. The question is one of loyalty. Shiny pointed out to me that he tried to hack into some Vovokan systems."

"He's Shiny's enemy?"

"Well, Shiny thought he should be on the team, actually," Cilreth admitted.

"This guy comes from Shiny?!" Imanol burst out.

"Back it down a notch," Magnus said. "I seem to recall you as being the abrasive one."

Cilreth laughed. "That's right, Imanol. You've rubbed a fair number of people the wrong way, too."

"I'm no traitor."

"Neither is he. He was hacking Shiny," Magnus said. "He was fighting the alien overlord that took over the Solar System. So he's loyal. We're the traitors. We work for Shiny."

"You know it's not that simple," Imanol said, but he had calmed down.

"Like she said, we'll watch him," Telisa said. "He's got what it takes to tackle alien systems and figure them out. How many times have we stared at something and we can't tell if it's an eating utensil or a death ray?"

Imanol looked to Magnus pleadingly. Magnus smiled.

"At least he's not a Trilisk," Magnus said. "Uhm, we did check to make sure he's not a Trilisk, right?"

"Right," Cilreth said.

"See? He's fine," Magnus said. Imanol rolled his eyes.

Magnus smiled. He enjoyed trivializing Imanol's concerns more than he thought he would. It felt good to be back.

Michael McCloskey

Chapter 27

Caden woke up so he could be ready for their arrival back at Rorka Cartur. Siobhan had shared his quarters last night, but as always, she fled to her own web to sleep. Caden had never figured out why, but he had learned to stop asking about it.

Maybe she sleeps upside down like a bat.

Within a few minutes of his rise, Siobhan showed up. She looked disheveled and tired. A yawn accented her condition. They showered in his tube and waited for news of the arrival.

"I'm awake now," she said.

"Ready for the probe ship again? I hope Shiny doesn't damage it, or piss of the Celarans."

"Exactly. How will he take it back?"

"Maybe he'll just raid it?" Caden said.

"He's more advanced. Maybe he can figure out their secrets faster than we could."

"The only other guess I have is that he might connect to the probe ship with his battleship and use its spinner to take both ships back to Earth immediately."

"We'll know soon."

He went off-retina to watch their arrival. They had started calling the massive Vovokan warship the *Rattler*, another joke based on the way Shiny communicated in his native format. Most of the PIT team felt that Shiny was not personally on board, but Telisa did not rule out the possibility of a Shiny clone commanding the ship.

The *Iridar* arrived first. A second later, the *Midway* resolved a few thousand kilometers away. Caden started looking for a viewpane with information from the sensor feeds.

"I don't have a feed," Siobhan said.

"Cthulhu sleeps!" exclaimed Cilreth.

"Something unexpected?" asked Siobhan.

"Yes. But there's no danger. The probe ship has left the system!"

"Are you sure?" Imanol asked. "It was cloaked well, right?"

"The attendants left behind watched it leave... after another cloaked ship arrived in the system!" Cilreth told them.

Caden thought of an immediate repercussion of the probe departure.

Telisa traded that thing for Magnus. And now it's gone. What's going to happen?

The *Rattler* arrived on their heels.

"Can we determine where it went?" Telisa demanded. Clearly she was way ahead of him. They needed to find that ship.

"I don't think so... wait a moment," Cilreth responded. "The attendants recorded a lot of information about the departures. Shiny's ship is sending me their course."

"I guess Vovokans can do that," Caden said. "Good to know."

"Yes, but *how*?" Siobhan asked.

"The remaining attendants have a message from an attendant that hitched a ride," Marcant said.

"Uhm, that makes no sense," Imanol said. "It has to be light years away."

"The attendants can send, but not receive, tachyonic messages, though to do so, they must sacrifice themselves," Marcant said.

"How could you possibly know that?" Imanol shot back. His voice sounded hostile.

"It came up in my research," Marcant said. "Cilreth is guiding my education about the Vovokans as you may recall."

Caden spoke to Siobhan aloud in his quarters. "Did you notice that? Does Marcant already know things Cilreth doesn't? He gave her credit for teaching him, but it sounded like maybe she didn't know how they did it."

"Maybe," Siobhan breathed. "It's good to have him though, unless Imanol is right not to trust him."

"Here's the new target," Marcant said. He shared a map to the system believed to be the destination of the probe ship.

"Shiny's ship is informing us of its intention to leave within the next few minutes," Cilreth said.

"Is that system on our list of Vovokan-discovered Celaran ruins?" asked Caden.

"No," Cilreth said.

"Just get ready for anything," Telisa said.

***

Marcant waded through another huge, goopy mess of yellow tentacles in the smelly water of the swamp. His legs felt leaden. Up ahead, he saw tall red reeds emerging from the water on his right and more yellow tentacles under the surface on his left.

"I say left side," Adair said. "The yellow ones disintegrate quickly. The red reeds get twisted around your legs and you'll have to stop to cut them again."

Marcant send a nonverbal acknowledgement and veered left.

Marcant had decided to train with Adair for now, since a defensive advisor seemed better suited to a newbie on the team. If he got better—much better—maybe he would let Achaius chime in. For now, he focused on following Adair's instructions.

"Stay low here," Adair said. "There's no reason to present a larger target than you have to."

"But I can barely move, and there's no enemy—"

The world exploded in smelly yellow water and broken reeds.

Marcant choked. For the next few seconds he struggled to orient himself. His Veer suit's helmet snapped shut and evacuated the slimy water as he coughed it up. Adair was speaking to him.

"Get behind that huge plant. Marcant, get behind that plant, you're being shot at."

"Caden, can you cover my left?" Siobhan said.

Marcant had dropped very low, leaving only the part of his helmet above his eyes protruding from the water. He looked left and right, then saw the tree. He took some steps toward it.

"Headed for the tree-thing. But why? I'm under cover now, isn't that what you wanted?" he said to Adair.

"Jason's been winged," Imanol said. "He can't move, but we can hold them off for a while. I still have three grenades."

"Look at the tactical," Adair said. "The enemy is to your 2 o'clock. The tree will cover you well and you can fire back from there. Not from underwater."

Marcant kept going. He saw on the tactical that Siobhan and Caden were at the focal point of a pincer movement by the enemy. All he really knew about those shooting at them was that they resembled "two-headed crocodiles".

He slogged to the wide, fat plant, which looked like a squashed willow tree with green anacondas for branches. He ran right into the branches, stopping with a wet slap, then dropped his rifle across one. He settled in nice and low, letting the tree conceal him. His barrel protruded through most of the tree.

"Okay, fire from here," Adair said.

Marcant started to shoot. He had a target profile which he fed to the rounds, though his rifle could not see the enemy. One of the creatures dropped off the tactical.

"I think I got one," he told Adair.

Siobhan went off the tactical, followed quickly by Jason. Imanol had joined Caden near the path of the left pincer force. Marcant fired several more times.

"They've moved on. We'll have to move forward to stay in range," Adair said. Marcant pulled his weapon out of the awful tree and started walking around it.

"We're taking heavy fire," said Imanol. Marcant slogged through another ten meters of swampy land. Then Imanol and Caden went offline. The simulation stopped. Marcant went on-retina in the lounge the team had been using to train near each other.

Imanol looked at Marcant.

Here we go.

"Why did you hold position once the attack started?" Imanol asked.

"The terrain was difficult. The tree was the best position anyway. Defensively, I mean," Marcant said.

"You left Siobhan out to dry."

"She was with Caden. I could fire from the tree at the enemy's right pincer force as they moved in on Siobhan and Caden."

Imanol scowled at Marcant.

"The entire team works as a unit," he said. "Just because Caden and Siobhan explore or patrol together does not mean they're on their own when something goes down. If any team member is in trouble, you stick your neck out to help them. Got it?"

"Yes," Marcant said. "Though before I died too easily, so I backed it off a bit."

Siobhan nodded. "I understand. Here's the deal. Be defensive initially, that's good. But if things get really bad despite that, it's time to take risks, because doing nothing kills us just as dead."

"It's time for dinner," Caden said. He did not sound angry. Marcant had learned to appreciate the little things.

Marcant rose with the others and headed for his quarters. He did not feel like hitting the mess at the same time as Imanol.

"Imanol looks for reasons to complain," Adair said. "It may just be a standard method to toughen you up."

"On the other hand, he has Magnus's ear," Achaius said.

"I'm sure he's complaining about me," Marcant said.

"He is," Achaius said. "Adair and I can still pick up their conversation from here."

Marcant stopped. His AIs piped the conversation in to him.

"He works for Shiny," Imanol was saying. "Shiny suggested him. The part about Marcant trying to hack Shiny was made up. This is all Shiny's doing. And those two AIs of his? Spheres. Who do we know that uses tiny spheres, medium spheres, and big battle spheres?"

Magnus frowned. "Not that suspicious. I've seen AIs housed in all kinds of chassis."

"You can bench him now. Use these exercises as an excuse. That way, no one dies for real."

"Think about it Imanol," Telisa said. "If it was a setup, he would show himself to be trustworthy in training, and betray us later. He stays on the team. When it's time to deploy incarnate, I'll give him something basic. We don't have to take him on dangerous patrols, his strength is in analysis."

Telisa is standing up for me.

Marcant sighed. "Damn. Now I have to repay her with loyalty."

Chapter 28

Marcant sat in his quarters, patiently awaiting their arrival at the next system. He mulled over his argument with Imanol. He knew he had been right and Imanol had been wrong, but had it been a mistake to stir up the team against him? Cilreth had told him that Imanol had annoyed everyone at one time or another, yet they seemed to stand up for Imanol now.

"The team has been together for a while," Adair said. "You have to wait for them to see your superiority themselves, you can't inform them of it."

"Then, half will respect you and half will hate you for it," Achaius said.

"I think you'd be right in most cases, Achaius," Marcant said. "But these people are intelligent and well adjusted. Telisa has chosen them well. Or perhaps it was Ambassador Shiny who chose them."

Before any reply could come, the *Iridar* broadcast an alert to its crew.

"Arrival at target system imminent," it said. A countdown timer feed appeared as the gravity spinner started to slow down. Marcant saw it would pass threshold energy in one hundred ship's seconds, dropping them into the system.

There was no need to go anywhere incarnate. Every feed and service was available to Marcant here in his quarters. Still, he donned his brand new Veer suit as a precaution.

"The others will either be happy with this or make fun of me when they see me in this outside of a training scenario," he said to Adair and Achaius.

"You're beyond the frontier now, this is appropriate garb," Adair encouraged. Marcant smiled. Adair, ever the cautious and defensive one, wanted him to sleep behind force fields and eat pre-scanned food every day. Of course it liked him in an armored suit.

Marcant put away the PV setup he had been using to study the Celaran artifacts and loaded a ship's interface set. The panes in his mind cleared away to make room for new ones. He saw all the non-private sections of the ship, an engineering summary including the state of the spinner, and the external sensor feeds. So far the external feeds were empty, and they would remain so until the spinner crossed the threshold in... ten seconds.

"We're here, people," Cilreth reported to the shared team channel.

Marcant saw the system tactical explode with information.

"Multiple ships! In fact—" Cilreth said.

"This is a combat situation!" Adair told Marcant.

"I can't make sense of it," Cilreth said.

"It's a fight," Magnus said. "And the *Rattler* has already joined in!"

Marcant watched objects accelerate away from the huge Vovokan warship. An electromagnetic readout also showed evidence that the ship fired energy weapons.

"Why would— Oh. Destroyers," Siobhan said.

Marcant saw the tactical resolve into different colors for ships as they were classified. The *Iridar* had already identified a group of Destroyer ships and innumerable Destroyer-related drones and ordinance in flight on defensive and offensive vectors. They appeared in red on his shared three-dimensional map, over a light minute away. Their own fleet, a paltry three ships, were displayed in green, vastly outnumbered in the system.

"There's the probe ship," Telisa said, marking an object on the tactical. "The other blue ships are the same; they must be Celaran."

The *Rattler* lit up as its shields dispersed energy. It was firing, but Marcant also saw reports of distress. Directed energy weapons were locked onto it.

"What are we doing?" Cilreth asked.

"Helping the Celarans, of course," Telisa said. "I've just told the *Midway* the same."

Marcant saw the *Midway* on the tactical. The *Rattler*, the *Midway*, and the *Iridar* had peeled away from each other and started to engage the Destroyers, though they were still very far away. Already a cloud of Destroyer ordinance could be seen leaving the enemy ships, headed for the newcomers.

"I can do better," Achaius told Marcant. "*Much* better."

Marcant opened a channel to Telisa and Cilreth.

"Cilreth, I beg you. Let me take control of the *Iridar*."

"What?"

"I can do better. I promise you, my fleet combat strategy is superior to my personal combat skills."

At first, Cilreth did not respond. Then she said, "I'm using the Vovokan routines. Obviously I'm not pulling every trigger myself."

"Yes, tactically the Vovokan routines are likely acceptable, but the *strategy*," Marcant said. "I can process everything we see out there, every single object, and come up with a course of action to optimize our impact in the battle."

"Telisa?"

"Your call, Cilreth," Telisa said.

"You know me. You recruited me. I can optimize this," Marcant said.

"I'll give you offensive and propulsion systems," Cilreth said. "I'll keep control of our defense."

Cilreth gave him the access he needed. Achaius went to it under Marcant's new link authorization. The lights dimmed and the artificial gravity disappeared. His crash tube lit up and beckoned his link.

"You will notice nonessential systems dropping off," Marcant said, simply to assuage the PIT team. He did not want to explain to them that Achaius would be conducting the battle on their behalf. They did not trust Marcant yet, Achaius, even less so, those that even knew about the AI. "Everyone shelter in your quarters or the central lounge. I'm going to cut some of the safety features elsewhere to save energy."

"Survival is not enough, it is imperative we support the Celarans in this fight," Telisa said.

"We don't command much firepower," Marcant said.

"Imperative, Marcant," Telisa maintained.

"Closing the range," Marcant said. Marcant told Achaius to comply.

"We've selected this target on the flank," Marcant said as Achaius worked. "This Vovokan ship has great speed and energy reserves, so we'll use that to our advantage. We should be able to snipe something and back off again before they can coordinate against us."

"Hurry. The *Rattler* is taking a beating. It won't be here to draw fire away from us for long," Magnus said.

"Agreed," Marcant said, though he did not really think much about it. Achaius already had the ship on an attack vector. The closer they approached, the less time each side had to react to incoming energy beams and ordinance. As Marcant watched, they closed to less than half a light minute apart.

Achaius directed the *Iridar* to launch an alpha strike at their chosen target. The energy reserves dropped quickly. Within seconds, the energy weapons had been fired. The *Iridar* released drones and counter-drones. Marcant would not know the results for many more seconds.

Are we going to die?

"Maybe yes," Adair said. It could read his thoughts with high accuracy. "There are too many factors out of our control here. We should have stayed home."

"We have a good chance of success," Achaius maintained.

The *Iridar* veered away unscathed. A small group of objects launched from the Destroyers behind and started to close on them. The tactical did not show Marcant what the objects were, meaning even Achaius probably did not know, but they were self-guided and accelerating. Marcant assumed they were missiles or attack drones. Whatever they were, he knew he did not want them to close with the *Iridar*.

"We've drawn their ire. I think our defenses will be up to it, though," Marcant said. The *Iridar* started to fire at its pursuers.

"Are those missiles or drones or what?" Telisa asked.

Before Marcant could answer, a message came in.

"This is the *Midway*. We're disengaging with heavy damage," Admiral Sager announced. "*Iridar*, can you lend us point defense?"

"Marcant, protect the *Midway*!" Telisa ordered.

"We may best look to our own survival—" Marcant started.

"Do it. The *Midway*!" Telisa insisted.

"Very well," Marcant said. The *Iridar* altered course to take up a vector trailing the *Midway*. Closing with *Midway* made *Iridar* take a course that let the pursuing Destroyer weapons edge closer.

Achaius altered course again. Instead of closing on the *Midway*, they were now headed closer to the objects locked on to the Space Force ship. The *Iridar* started to shoot at Destroyer objects headed for *Midway*. They managed to destroy half of them in one large energy weapon salvo, but the remaining ones changed course for the *Iridar*.

The only good thing Marcant saw now was that they also neared the *Rattler*.

"If we can't handle these missiles, how can we handle ours AND theirs?" Cilreth asked.

"Everyone's a back seat driver," Achaius said to Marcant.

"The Celarans have rallied," Magnus said. "If we die, they can't say Terrans never did them a favor."

"You're hoping Shiny's battleship can protect us?" Telisa asked.

"No, it's almost dead. In fact—" Marcant was cut off as the *Rattler* started to break up before them in a series of massive explosions. Matter from the ship shot outwards in an expanding envelope of debris. Achaius headed straight for the calamity.

"We're dead," Magnus said.

They headed into the field of debris. Instead of firing rearward at their pursuers, the *Iridar* started to fire forward to shatter objects large enough to destroy it before they struck. The *Iridar* made it through the wavefront without damage. The pursuing Destroyer weapons lit up behind them as they locked on to pieces of the *Rattler* and detonated.

"Good job," Telisa said. "I'm impressed."

"That was amazing, many thanks," sent Sager.

Marcant basked in the praise in Achaius's place. "You hear that? They love us," Marcant said to his AIs.

"This large enemy ship has targeted us. We don't have anything that can stop its energy weapons," Achaius said. It pointed out a route through the *Iridar* in Marcant's PV.

"This ship has an escape pod," Adair said to Marcant. "It's time to use it."

Marcant struggled for a moment.

Surely I should act to preserve myself?

A new object appeared on the tactical. At first Marcant saw it as the beginning of a massive launch by the

Destroyer ship. Then, it changed from gray to blue on the screen. A pane opened for it.

"A Celaran ship just became visible at point blank range to that Destroyer ship!" Cilreth said. By the time she had completed her sentence, a flower of energy grew to envelop the area of space the Destroyer ship had occupied.

"I think they got it," Marcant said. "Yes, they did. And they're still alive!"

"*Midway*, turn around. We need to group up with that ship and clean up the enemy."

"Understood," Admiral Sager replied.

Wow. That admiral hops to it when Telisa gives an order. Even with his ship burning around him.

Marcant brought the *Iridar* to a course parallel to the Celaran ship. The *Midway* limped along behind, unable to match their acceleration. The blue Celaran ship on the tactical did nothing for a moment, then it adjusted course, slowly coming around to engage the last cluster of three Destroyer ships.

The Destroyers all decided to fire on the Celaran ship. Its shields coruscated, then it started to veer away.

"They're killing the Celarans! Quick, do something!" Telisa ordered. A part of Marcant knew her urgings were almost useless, yet he did not blame her for saying it. He had almost yelled the same thing himself.

Iridar charged forward and expended its energy weapons on the biggest Destroyer of the three. The ship took the hit but did not explode.

Damn, now we're in trouble again!

The *Iridar* changed course crazily to avoid incoming energy bursts. Behind them, the *Midway* finally fired. At the vast distances, everything was so slow. Marcant counted the seconds, waiting to see the result. After fifteen seconds, the weakened ship of the enemy blossomed into light and debris.

"We're doing it! We're winning!" Telisa said.

The surviving Destroyers did not break off. The two small ships tried to fire on the *Midway*, but they were clearly shooting on generated energy. They had no stored energy left to throw into it. The Celaran vessel closed on one of the enemy and finished them off. *Iridar* tried to do the same, but it was also out of energy. Achaius launched ten drones at the Destroyer ship, then dropped energy to the gravity spinner to recharge. The enemy ship tried to evade the drones, but it had nothing left. After a twenty second chase, the lead drone caught up to the enemy and destroyed it.

"That's it. We've done it," Siobhan exalted.

"They'll be our friends now, surely?" Cilreth said.

"I'm returning power to all ship's systems," Marcant said.

"Cthulhu's minions," Cilreth breathed. She did not sound happy.

"What is it?" Telisa asked.

Cilreth did not respond. Caden solemnly answered for her. "Check the crew vitals."

"Someone died!" Jason exclaimed.

Marcant did not believe him at first. He checked the ship. Everyone showed up on the crew status viewpane except... Imanol.

"Imanol is not in his quarters," Marcant said slowly.

"In the port armory," Cilreth said. "My attendants found him. I'm sorry... he's very dead."

"How could it have happened? That's near the center of the ship. We weren't hit, were we?" Caden asked.

"He wasn't in his quarters," Marcant repeated. As soon as he said it, he realized exactly what had happened. Marcant had blocked communication with Imanol in anger after the last argument. When he had warned everyone to shelter in their quarters or the central lounge, Imanol had not received the warning.

I killed Imanol.

Attendants flew around the room, scanning the remains. The feed was available. Marcant made himself look. Imanol had been crushed during the veer off from their first pass at the Destroyers. The ship had run low on energy and allowed the gravity spinner to eddy into parts of the ship that were not supposed to be occupied. It had either been a lack of acceleration compensation from their energetic maneuver, or a violent eddy of the spinner that had killed Imanol.

It was... most efficient to use every joule of energy only where it was needed. All our lives were on the line.

Marcant felt an odd emotion run through him. He had been so angry at Imanol just a short time ago. Now the man was dead.

"And they'll think you did it on purpose," Adair said.

"This could be a problem," Achaius agreed. They both sounded as somber as he had ever heard them.

Of course Adair and Achaius were right. The PIT team would suspect it was no accident. Marcant left his quarters and marched to the armory incarnate.

When he got there, he saw Telisa and Cilreth standing at the door, looking over the carnage. Imanol's bones were still recognizable, though the rib cage had crumpled. Marcant felt dizzy for a moment.

Telisa did not shed tears, but her face showed pain. Caden showed up, followed by Siobhan. Siobhan gasped and made a pathetic noise.

"Clean this up," Telisa ordered. Her voice was firm.

Marcant waited for an accusation. He saw Caden make the realization. Caden turned away from the gore to look at Marcant.

Might as well bite the bullet.

"I did not do this on purpose," Marcant said. "I offer a truth check."

"Passing a truth check would be child's play for a man like you," Caden said.

"Enough!" Telisa snapped. "Marcant saved us. *I'll* worry about whether or not Imanol was murdered. The rest of you, focus on the Celarans. Some of them survived. We need to meet them face to face and learn to communicate."

"*Iridar*, this is *Midway*. Captain Relachik, are you there?"

"We are, minus one casualty," Telisa responded.

"We lost many more," Sager replied. "My assessment of our condition is grim. At least we've stabilized the situation here."

"We will assist you with repairs," Telisa said.

"Thank you. What's after that?" Sager asked.

"Next, we meet our allies," Telisa said.

Chapter 29

"Do we really want to meet them face to face?" Caden asked. Everyone sat in a large lounge, trying to gather themselves after the battle and the loss of their companion. Awful suspicions about Marcant ran through Siobhan's mind, but she trusted Telisa to figure out what had happened. In the meantime, the Celarans were only a few thousand kilometers away.

"That's the only way," Telisa said. "We can't interface with their systems, remember? A virtual meeting is impossible. That is, unless you and Siobhan made the necessary critical breakthroughs on Celaran technology during the battle."

Caden and Siobhan traded sullen looks.

We couldn't figure it out. Maybe Marcant can, if he didn't kill Imanol, Siobhan thought.

"Okay, then. Cilreth has us on a gentle rendezvous course with the largest Celaran ship that survived the battle. *Midway* is keeping its distance."

"Wait a minute. Didn't the—" Jason started.

"The Earth ambassador was among their many casualties," Telisa said. "It's up to us now."

"How long until we meet that ship?" Caden asked.

"Less than an hour. Clean yourselves. Sterilize, more like. I want no odors. Be careful with lights and lasers, we believe they communicate with light. No weapons."

"So we're just going to walk over there and say hi?" Marcant asked. "I knew this was dangerous, but I hoped for more... calculated risks."

"This is the least risky thing I'll ever ask you to do," Telisa said. "We went into a Celaran complex and their security machines never seriously harmed us. The same happened with the probe ship. They let Blackvines live in peace inside their space habitat. Can you imagine what would happen to an alien trespassing on a Space Force base?"

"The Space Force would shoot first," Caden said.

"Everything has pointed to the Celarans being peaceful. We just fought a battle on their side. The risk is *low*, people."

That shut everyone up. Despite the speech, Telisa's nerves were frazzled by the loss of Imanol. Siobhan could see it. Still, that didn't shake her confidence in Telisa. It just meant that Telisa really cared.

"Everyone is just contemplating their mortality again, seeing Imanol die like that," Caden sent Siobhan privately.

"Understood. But it's time to step up. This is a momentous occasion," Siobhan told him.

"We're going to make contact with the Celarans," Telisa said. "We'll cement a friendship that will last a long time. Then we'll have an ally against the Destroyers, and... against Shiny, if it comes to that."

"What if one of them is a Trilisk?" Siobhan asked.

Telisa stared at Siobhan for a moment.

"Cilreth, get ready to scan them for traces of Trilisk activity," Telisa said. "If we find evidence that one of them is a Trilisk, we'll act ignorant of that fact and slowly go back to *Iridar* after trading a few gifts. Did I mention the gifts yet?"

"How do we know they like gifts?" Jason said.

"We don't. But, they might help us understand each other. They can analyze our tech and we might get some more of theirs to look at. Anything that might help us communicate."

"How will we connect to their ship? Do we know we can breathe their air?" Jason asked.

"This ship is flexible. It can already connect to both Vovokan and Terran ships and habitats. If I know the Celarans, their airlock connections will be even more flexible... they're the supreme re-users, remember?

Everything they make does like five things. Expect something similar to what we found on the probe. As for the air, we've already been to two planets they put colonies on. I think we'll be fine, and if not, we can use the Veer suits' masks."

Siobhan left the group to get ready for the rendezvous.

No weapons, but that doesn't mean I can't have a trick up my sleeve, just in case.

Siobhan put on her stealth suit. She realized that trapped inside an alien spaceship, it might not be enough, but it calmed her nerves.

Telisa is right. They're peaceful.

Soon the call came for everyone to assemble. Telisa sent out a message indicating the lock they would use. Everyone showed up quickly except Cilreth, which did not surprise Siobhan. No doubt Cilreth would mind the ship during the meeting.

"Just so you know, I'm sharing a feed with the *Midway*," Telisa sent out on the team channel. "Move slowly. No one so much as twitch. We know their machines are very tolerant, and they probably are too, but I don't want to make them nervous," Telisa said.

Their machines might escalate to violence a lot faster with real Celarans to protect, Siobhan thought. She realized her pulse was elevated.

Siobhan watched a video feed from outside the *Iridar* as they sidled up to the alien ship. As different as the Celarans were, they shared the concept of an airlock with the Terrans. It was hexagonal in shape, but the *Iridar* would be able to make an airtight seal against the other hull around the lock.

A Vovokan attendant hovered at the door, ready to leave the *Iridar* first.

"The seal is ready," Cilreth reported. Telisa told the airlock to open. Siobhan held Caden's hand for a moment, then she released it so she could be ready for anything.

The attendant entered the lock and let the door cycle behind it.

"I'm going to give them plenty of time to decide it's harmless," Telisa said.

The attendant floated in the tunnel between the ships for a couple of minutes. Siobhan started to feel impatient to go over and take a look herself.

Caden and I would already be in there. I suppose that's why Telisa is in charge.

Caden traded a look with Siobhan that meant he knew exactly what she was thinking. She smiled back at him.

At last the Celaran hatch opened. A small disk-shaped machine came out of their ship. It was smaller than the attendant. Unlike the slow-moving, hovering attendant, the disk flew about playfully.

"Ah, we'll let that in now," Telisa said. Everyone backed up against the wall in the corridor to make room for the Celaran machine to fly in and look around. The *Iridar*'s lock opened to let the machine inside. Siobhan watched the feed from the attendant as it entered the Celaran ship at almost the same moment.

The Celaran's flying scout came into the *Iridar* and hovered before Telisa. Their leader stood erect and allowed the tiny machine to get a good look. Siobhan used her combat skills to divide her attention between the little flying machine and the video feed from their own attendant. The things she saw from the attendant quickly became much more interesting.

Siobhan expected the inside of the Celaran ship to have larger spaces than a Terran vessel, but she still felt shock when she saw the feed from the attendant.

The entire ship is one big open space!

At least a dozen Celarans hung inside on wall rods. Three fingers at one end clasped the rod, then their two-meter long bodies hung outwards toward the center of the ship. They looked just like larger versions of the feral snakelike flyers they had seen on the planet, except they wore the harnesses or clothing as Cilreth had figured out. The Celarans were restless, always moving, swinging, or curling their bodies.

Maybe that's a sign of excitement?

"That's crazy," Magnus said.

"It's just like the space habitat," Cilreth said.

"And the hangars we found on the planet," said Caden. "Look, their bodies are pointed—"

"Toward the center!" Telisa finished. "Though the attendant reports very low acceleration, less than a third of a G."

"Wouldn't they want the gravity pulled outwards, as if the walls of the ship were the ground?" Siobhan wondered.

"And can they really afford to waste that much volume? If the hull is breached then there's no way to mitigate the loss of air," Magnus said.

"This is their way," Telisa said. "I'm sure it's no waste to them. And they survived the battle."

Siobhan thought about what Magnus had said. If this ship had been hit by a fragment from the battle and pierced the hull, there would be no segmentation structure to stop the loss of the atmospheric pressure. Why would they risk that?

"They must have rapid repair systems, advanced shields, possibly each crewmember can protect themselves from vacuum," she thought aloud.

"Ready? Here we go," Telisa said. She added a bit more over the channel so Cilreth could hear: "Watch our little flying guest just in case."

"Will do," Cilreth sent back. "Good luck."

"Two at a time in the tunnel," Telisa ordered. Magnus entered the tunnel with her. Caden and Siobhan beat out Jason for the next pair. Jason looked dismal and Siobhan knew it was not because he was last; it was because Imanol was dead.

The Celaran robot had flown into every open space of the *Iridar*. Siobhan wondered if it noticed any inconsistencies stemming from the Terrans being in a Vovokan ship.

It's like when we found the Blackvines living in a Celaran habitat. We had no idea for a long time.

Telisa had arrived in the Celaran ship. A Celaran floated near the door, only two meters away from her now. Siobhan imagined it was there to welcome them, though she knew that was a very Terran assumption.

"By the Five, it's beautiful," Telisa said. Siobhan and Caden started across the tunnel, watching the video feed from ahead.

The Celaran wore a black and blue harness across its long, flat body like the ones they had found in the ruins. It floated down to the level of the Terrans before it. The creature's many chevrons shimmered with bright color across its otherwise black skin. It was a living, flickering iridescent light.

It's saying something.

"It's larger than the ones we saw before!" Siobhan said over the shared channel.

The Celaran abruptly slid away through the air. Its flat body undulated like the fins of an eel. Siobhan noticed it fold the three fingers on each end of its body down against its underside for flight. Siobhan remembered that its clothing probably had tech to help it move as well.

"It moves surprisingly fast," Magnus said. The tone of his voice suggested an appraisal of the danger it posed.

Telisa floated a bit farther inside to make room for the others. She moved very slowly. Then she started to fall toward the center of the ship, so she had an attendant nudge her toward the nearest hanging bar. Once there, Telisa hooked her lower legs around the bar and let her upper body float toward the center of the ship in the light gravity.

"When in Rome..." Telisa said with a smile. Siobhan smiled too. She felt genuinely happy until she recalled the crewmember who had not lived to see this.

Jason and Marcant came across, then all the Terrans hooked their lower legs around the rods at the knee and hung with the Celarans. The low gravity ensured that it was not uncomfortable for them to hang "upside down", with the blood rushing to their heads.

"I'm sure we look ridiculous, not only to the folks on the *Midway*, but also to the Celarans," Siobhan sent Caden privately. He just grinned and kept watching the Celarans.

"We're going to need some fancy light emitters and recorders," Telisa said. "For starters, we should record their flickering and play it back for them, to let them know we're aware that's how they speak."

"Your flashlights can do it, at least for part of the spectrum," Marcant said. "Record from your links. Shall I try?"

"Yes," Telisa ordered.

Marcant released his hanging rod and floated forward under the power of his attendant. He detached a light from his suit and held it forward. It flickered in several colors. Immediately a Celaran glided forward to see it up close. It came so quickly that Marcant looked startled.

They're fast. Very fast.

"Let's hope they sense at least part of the same light spectrum we do," Siobhan said.

The Celaran clearly responded. It flashed bright red and held it, then bright blue. Marcant repeated the sequence, at least the part of it in the spectrum visible to Terrans.

"It knows we know that it's talking," Telisa said. "And I'm sure it can tell from how lame our lights are that we don't know how to say anything that way."

"The light patterns they use are sophisticated. I now also ascribe to your theory that this is their primary method of communication," Marcant said imperiously.

"Good," Telisa said. "Marcant, it's on you. I want to talk to them. Figure it out." Telisa's voice was harder than usual.

It's like she's making it clear, Marcant needs to prove he's worth everything that's happened, Siobhan thought.

Marcant stared at Telisa for a moment as if trying to check for a joke.

"Understood," Marcant finally said calmly enough, but his composure cracked just a little bit.

And try not to kill anyone, Siobhan silently added.

Made in the USA
Middletown, DE
10 January 2023